Never Mind Miss Fox

OLIVIA GLAZEBROOK

virago

VIRAGO

First published in Great Britain in 2014 by Virago Press

Copyright © 2014 by Olivia Glazebrook

The moral right of the author has been asserted.

*All characters and events in this publication, other than those
clearly in the public domain, are fictitious and any resemblance
to real persons, living or dead, is purely coincidental.*

A CIP catalogue record for this book
is available from the British Library.

ISBN 978-1-84408-941-3

Typeset in Garamond by M Rules
Printed and bound in Great Britain by
Clays Ltd, St Ives plc

Papers used by Virago are from well-managed forests
and other responsible sources.

MIX
Paper from
responsible sources
FSC
www.fsc.org   FSC® C104740

Virago Press
An imprint of
Little, Brown Book Group
100 Victoria Embankment
London EC4Y 0DY

An Hachette UK Company
www.hachette.co.uk

www.virago.co.uk

'Hey, Mum? Guess what.'

'You know I'll never guess,' said Martha. 'What?'

Eliza swung her rucksack on to one shoulder and pulled her ponytail over the other. 'My new piano teacher knows you,' she said, 'and she knows Dad too.'

Clive was undressing when Martha told him.

'The oddest thing,' she began. 'You'd never guess in a thousand years.' Then she went back to cleaning her teeth and he heard brushing, spitting, rinsing and sluicing.

Clive pulled off his trousers and sat on the corner of the bed. He waited, yawning, and then called after her into the bathroom. 'For God's sake – what?'

Martha came to the bedroom door and looked down at him. In one hand she held a reel of dental floss. 'Eliza's got a new piano teacher,' she said, 'and it's Eliot Fox.'

Part I

1

Clive fell in love with Martha at Oxford, in the final days of their last spring term. Realising her worth – afraid to leave her unattended – he begged her to join his family's annual Easter trip to France. 'It's very relaxed,' he lied. 'We can do what we like and' – the trump card – 'my parents will pay for everything.'

Martha agreed at once: 'I love France, and I love families.' She was studying French and Arabic, and she had no family of her own. 'I do have a father,' she told Clive. 'Aiden Doyle? He's a writer.' Clive shook his head but because he loved her he searched through shelves of second-hand books until he found one – *Wild Bird Calling* – to take on holiday.

Martha's reputation – she was described by various sources as a 'stroppy cow', 'a slag' and 'a laugh' – had kept Clive at a distance and in the end she had dealt with the matter herself: she had kissed him in a pub corridor, between the toilets and the bar, and pressed him against the wall with a glorious, winning confidence.

To her evident surprise the kiss had been both revelatory and full of promise. She had pulled away and stared at his face in delight, as if she had not really looked at it before – as perhaps she had not. 'Well I never,' she had murmured, smiling. She had let her hands rest on his shoulders and leaned her hips against his until he would have done anything – anything – to keep her there.

Clive had never been in love before and he soon discovered that its terrors were at least as numerous as its pleasures. He could not bear to surrender this precious treasure over the Easter break, and he would have told her a pack of lies to make her come away. As it turned out, she was willing to come for something near enough the truth.

Peter and Val Barkes had discovered their 'adorably backward' French seaside town in the first years of their marriage and returned every year since. Their two sons, Clive and Tom, had played on the beach with buckets and spades, learned to swim in salted, lapping shallows and wobbled their bicycles along quiet lanes which wound between shifting, whispering dunes. It was only in recent years – since a budget airline had pounced on the local airport – that the resort had begun to be saturated by holidaymakers of a different type, whom Peter christened 'the hordes'. These visitors, oafish and insensitive, had spoiled everything.

The whole place was pronounced 'ruined' but Peter and Val continued to visit, coming at Easter to avoid the summer crowds. 'We won't be chased away,' they said. 'We found it first.' This year, however, a heatwave brought an unexpected tide of tourists and the couple would not be consoled: first the town and now the climate had turned against them.

'It's global whatsit,' said Val, fanning herself with a laminated menu. 'It's too hot; it's not right.'

'What did your parents talk about in the old days?' Martha asked Clive. 'Before climate change and mass tourism?'

Tom and his friend Eliot both laughed when they heard this but Clive was embarrassed. He was frightened of Martha's judgement and began to see his parents with a keen, peeled gaze. No longer were they 'Mum and Dad' but now, 'Peter and Val'. What he saw – what he thought Martha saw – made him shrivel. 'My parents are being awful,' he apologised. 'I don't know what's got into them. They're not normally as bad as this.'

'They're not awful,' said Martha in surprise. 'They're lovely. Your mum is such a *Mum* – she's like the one in the ad for Fairy Liquid.'

Clive did not know whether this was a good or bad thing. In reply to something she might have meant he said, 'It's not short for Valerie, by the way. It's short for Valentine.'

When she heard this Martha laughed at him and said, 'You are funny.'

Clive had not meant to be funny. Worry made him tense; tension – or perhaps a bad oyster – made him sick. He lay in bed, wretched, clutching his knotted stomach.

'Are you ill?' asked Martha, looking down at him in the bed as she rubbed sunscreen into her face. She did not seem sympathetic, and Clive wondered if she had heard him in the bathroom, during the night.

It occurred to him that they did not know each other well enough for bouts of vomiting and diarrhoea in the same small space. 'I'll be better in an hour or so,' he said. 'You go on, to the beach.'

When she had gone he dragged himself to the *pharmacie* but could not bear to mime his symptoms and make himself understood. He returned to the hotel bathroom and hunched over the toilet to retch and weep. *This is not fair*, he thought afterwards, blowing his nose and gargling Listerine. He curled up on the floor around the bidet and remained there in a doze, waking now and again to wonder if anyone was missing him.

He was roused by a knock at the door and a shrill voice: Eliot's. 'Your mum sent me to find out whether you're ill. Are you? Clive? Hello?' She barged in and saw him on the floor. 'Shit,' she said. 'You look awful.'

Tom had said of Eliot, 'I'm bringing a girl but she's not my girl-friend, just my friend.' It was obvious he loved her, but not that she loved him. 'You can put us in the same room, Mum,' Tom had said in a gloomy voice. 'She won't even snog me. I've tried everything.'

Val's zipped-purse mouth almost disappeared when she heard this. 'May I remind you,' she said, 'that it's not only drinking and smoking you and your *friend* are too young for. You may think you're very grown-up but in my eyes – not to mention the eyes of the law – you're both children.'

'It's ironic really,' Tom mused to Clive. 'Most of the girls at my school are slags – much slaggier than the ones at the comp – but this one won't even kiss me for a fiver.'

'Too bloody rich,' was Martha's comment.

Tom had won a scholarship to school in London, a fact which never ceased to irritate Clive. 'Why do you care?' Martha said to him. 'Public school is for dickheads.'

'Slags and dickheads,' corrected Tom.

Now Eliot peeled Clive off the bathroom floor and marched him to the chemist. 'You've got to sort yourself out,' she said. 'It's not sexy to be ill – especially with bum-related stuff.' In a torrent of schoolgirl French she demanded medicine and swapped Clive's money for two packets of pills. 'One's for the squits,' she said, 'and the other's for constipation. You can do the fine-tuning.'

Clive took the paper bag from her and returned to his room.

He got up late in the afternoon and judged himself recovered enough to go to the beach. One of the landmarks of ruination noted by Peter and Val was a brand new ('monstrous') concrete toilet block, squatting beside the Café du Soleil. Today it might make itself useful.

Standing on the sand, wobbly and alone, Clive looked at the happy scene before him and realised with a sinking heart that those few short hours in bed had cost him his place in the group. Martha, Eliot and Tom were fooling around like three young kids; his parents were shepherding them with indulgent good humour. Adult conversation had been replaced by offers of ice-cream and reminders about sunscreen; the kids – 'You kids!' – did nothing but giggle, cheat at *pétanque* and try to push each other over on the sand.

Clive hovered at the edge of the game, uncertain. Martha had last night been his ally but this person before him, laughing with Tom, was a stranger. Her bare, sandy legs were planted wide apart on the beach and a rope of hair swung on her back. She looked as assertive, unguarded and free as a pony turned loose in a field.

Clive felt abandoned and out of his depth. He did not approve of giggles, which did not sound to him like laughter, but when she saw him Martha said, 'Clive! You're better!' in such an artless, cheerful voice he thought it must be all right.

'Just about,' said Clive. 'I feel pretty awful.'

He knew that Eliot was right and that while fortitude was sexy, illness was not. He knew what he should have said: 'Much better! Can I join in?' But he preferred not to help himself. He watched Martha drop her hand and turn away, and he felt the pleasant, seeping satisfaction of the victim.

'Rotten luck,' his father sympathised. 'I expect it was an oyster. The sea's not as clean as it used to be back in the day.'

'That's such crap, Dad,' called Tom. 'You don't know what you're talking about. We used to swim through shoals of floating turds, me and Clive, when we were kids.'

Peter pretended not to have heard and Val said, 'Please, Tom,' in a faint voice.

Clive stood for a little longer and then sideways, crab-like, approached his mother's folding chair and crouched beside it. 'Tomorrow,' he said, 'why don't we all do our own thing? You and Dad could go and look at a château or something – get away from us lot for the day.'

'We're not here to do our own thing,' said Val in surprise. 'We're here on a family holiday – and anyway I love "you lot". That wicked little Eliot makes me laugh, and your girlfriend's bottom is doing wonders for your father – do look, Clive, he's gone absolutely scarlet.'

But Clive did not look; he could not laugh; he would not relax.

Before dinner he lay on his hotel bed and listened to his brother and Eliot chattering to each other on their balcony. Martha was in the shower and Clive did not want her to hear them. Something had gone wrong, something untraceable, and it made him get to his feet and slide shut the balcony door.

Martha came back into the room naked, rosy and hot. Her hair was bundled up in a towel. 'It still stinks in there,' she said. 'Why have you shut the door? It's so hot.'

'The other two were making a racket.'

Martha pulled the towel off her head and turned herself upside down to rub at her wet hair. 'Are they shagging?' she asked.

'Shagging?' said Clive, shocked. 'No, they're talking.'

'Talking!' Martha uprighted herself and mocked him. 'How outrageous!'

'It was the smoke,' said Clive. 'The cigarette smoke was coming in. I'm feeling ill, remember?'

'How could I forget,' she teased, coming over to the bed and clambering up beside him.

Clive felt a flash of hot temper. 'Get off, will you?' he said. 'I'm not in the mood.'

Martha stopped where she was, prowling across the coverlet to reach him, and sat back on her heels. 'Now that you mention it,' she said, 'neither am I.' She retreated off the bed, got dressed, and left the room without another word.

Clive decided that if only Eliot would get off with Tom, he and Martha would be all right again. He tried to encourage the romance the next day.

'I do love Tom,' said Eliot, cycling along the sea road beside Clive, 'but not like that. It's not going to happen; I've told him a million times. Anyway, I'm in love with Mr Lennox.'

'Who's he?'

'My piano teacher. Really – I'm not joking: I love him.'

'You're being ridiculous,' said Clive. 'That's not going to happen.' Her crush distressed him. *Perhaps*, he thought, *I am protective of Tom*. 'Your teacher won't think of you like that,' he tried to persuade her, 'trust me.'

'You underestimate my feminine wiles,' Eliot replied. 'You don't know what it's like: sitting next to each other at the piano, all cooched up and cosy, nothing but music, him telling me where to put my hands ...' Sticking her nose in the air she pedalled away from him, laughing.

Clive watched her go – salted hair sticking straight up, a smut of freckles across her nose, torn-off denim shorts of Tom's and sandy feet in plimsolls – and he wondered.

'What does she want to happen?' he asked Martha. 'Sex? With her piano teacher?'

'Not sex,' said Martha. 'Love.'

This was right; Clive believed her. Eliot did not want to have sex with Mr Lennox but she wanted him to love her best – more than he loved his wife, his children and his job. So much, in fact, that he would abandon everything and risk imprisonment: run away with her like Humbert Humbert, to live in a bedsit in a rainy town beside the sea.

The fantasy was absurd and Clive was prepared to bet that if any part of it had encroached on her reality Eliot would have been frightened and revolted. She loved and she longed to be loved, but the real thing when it came – Tom's wholehearted gift of himself, inside and out – was unattractive. She wanted something more painful and vicious: someone who did not want her.

Peter and Val admired Martha but they adored Eliot. She bowled them over. 'That girl,' chuckled Peter, 'is a real charmer. She's got pizazz.'

Val was protective. 'I hope she's going to be all right.' To Tom she said, 'You must look out for Eliot, Tom. She's just the type to get mixed up in silly nonsense; she doesn't take care of herself.'

'She cares about her hands,' said Tom.

This was true. 'They're the only part of me that's any use,' Eliot said, looking down at them.

One night she played the piano for them in the lobby. She stood in front of them and announced, 'This is a sonata in D major by Scarlatti. You can clap at the end, but not in the middle.' She frowned – serious, for once – and then sat down and lifted her hands.

Afterwards she boasted to Tom, 'Now I can make your

parents do anything I want, you watch.' It was true: before they could gather their wits she had persuaded Val and Peter to get up the next morning at the crack of dawn and drive the whole party – yawning like kittens – to a town famous for its *marché aux puces*.

The outing was like an unexpected day off from school due to flooding or snowfall. The structure of the group disintegrated – to Clive's relief – and for the duration of the morning they were not a family but a gathering of six runaways.

Val could not stop giggling. 'It's getting up early,' she apologised, laying a tipsy hand on Martha's arm. 'It makes me light-headed.' She insisted that everyone eat breakfast – hot chocolate and croissants in the town square – and that Peter give them holiday money to spend in the market.

'Petty cash?' said Peter. 'I'm not sure I can spare it—'

'Oh, *Pe*-ter,' said Val, taking his wallet from him and distributing the notes.

'Right,' said Peter, regaining the ascendancy, 'this is the assembly point. We'll reconvene at noon.'

At the appointed hour Val appeared carrying a bird cage and Martha a penknife, 'For my dad'. Eliot had bought herself an old khaki jacket, ex-army, covered with pockets and smelling like a wet marquee. It was too big but she put it on and did not take it off. 'I've always wanted one of these,' she said. 'Do you think someone died in it? Can you see any blood?' She searched each pocket for clues.

Tom produced from his pocket a brooch – a gold-and-black-enamelled bee with a spark of diamanté in each eye – which he wrapped in a napkin and gave to Eliot. She was speechless, turning it in her hands. She put both arms around his neck and kissed him a delighted thank you, saying, 'You're adorable. It's the nicest thing that's happened to me ever.'

Clive had found nothing he wanted and had returned his father's money. Now he was furious: his brother had shamed him in front of Martha. 'That must have cost you double,' he snapped at Tom. 'You've broken the rules – so typical.'

'Hush, Clive,' said Val. 'We've all had a lovely time. Don't spoil it.' She patted Eliot on the knee. 'Thank you, dear, for bringing us – it was such a good idea to come.'

But now Martha was offended. Why had Clive not bought her anything? She snatched at Eliot's buoyant mood with teeth bared. 'Aren't you hot,' she asked her, 'in that jacket? You must be roasting.' She said it several times.

To hear that tone of voice made Clive's heart sink. Eliot and Tom – bold, curious, light-headed and silly – had reminded Martha that life used to be more fun. 'I think I've had enough of Miss Fox for about the next thousand years,' she said to Clive. 'She's a cocky little brat, and your parents have been completely taken in.' Eliot had annoyed her, Peter and Val had disappointed her, and Clive had failed her. He heard the accusation in her voice; he heard his stomach gurgle; he wanted to go home.

Peter and Val's routine had been upset by the trip to the market and at lunchtime they forgot their usual strictness. Eliot drank Campari, and Tom two glasses of beer. 'All kids drink in France, Dad,' said Tom. 'It's the norm.' He burped. 'Normageddon.'

His mother pursed her lips but did not remonstrate. Even when Eliot wheedled a cigarette out of her jacket and lit it Val said only, 'Dear child – do have a care for your poor little lungs.'

In the car on the way back to their hotel Val snorted, woke with a start and yawned. 'I'm pooped,' she said, and put a hand on Peter's knee. 'Why don't we have room service and an early night,' she asked him, 'as a treat?'

Ranked behind him in the two back rows of the people mover – 'It's a type of car, Dad,' Clive had sneered at the rental kiosk. 'Don't you even know that?' – Eliot and Tom started giggling and Clive shrank with shame. Martha, sulking, gave no sign of having heard.

At the hotel Peter and Val seemed elderly and incapable. 'I'm all at sixes and sevens,' said Val in a worried voice. 'It's the early start, and wine at lunchtime.' Peter collected their room key and steered his wife upstairs.

Martha went to telephone her father. 'I haven't spoken to him since I left,' she accused Clive.

Tom sidled up to Clive and asked him to order drinks which he and Eliot could have upstairs. 'They won't serve us,' Tom said. 'The staff, I mean. I think Dad must have told them not to.'

Clive rang down to the kitchen. Minutes later an unsmiling waiter delivered two bottles of red wine on a tray. His disgust was palpable. Clive paid him in cash, too frightened to ask for change, and the waiter took a slow moment to fold the notes into his waistcoat pocket before he withdrew.

14

Tom whisked in through the balcony door. '*Merci, monsieur*,' he said in a camp voice, picking up the tray. He was over-excited; he thought Eliot might kiss him tonight.

Clive fretted. He got into the shower and worried there, lathering his head, and then lay on the counterpane and turned the pages of his book. Martha did not return.

When he woke up later – stiff, cold and only half-covered by a damp towel – she was asleep beside him, her back as uncompromising as a sandbag. Clive stared at her shape and wondered what had woken him. There was a noise; lifting his head from the pillow he saw Tom, stepping into the room from their shared balcony.

'Tom?'

'Help – Clive – help – quick –'

Martha was awake – entirely awake – at once. 'What is it?' she said, sitting up and switching on the light. Clive flinched and blinked; his head felt dim; he was confused.

Tom said, 'Eliot keeps being sick' – his voice fluttered with panic – 'and she won't stop. Please – come – quick –'

Martha pushed the bedclothes back and got up in her pants. She picked up a vest from the floor and pulled it on. 'How much has she drunk?' she asked, already following Tom through the open door.

'I don't know,' said Tom and then added, miserably, 'She just kept downing it.'

Clive got to his feet, fumbled into a T-shirt and shorts and went after them.

All the lights blazed in the next-door room and a bitter,

stewed smell of vomited alcohol made his throat smart and his stomach clench. Eliot had been sick all over the bedclothes and in a splatter on the carpet. Claret-coloured stains bloomed on the sheets; chunks of food were glued to the skirting board. Now she was propped against the door frame between bedroom and bathroom, flopping sideways like a worn-out teddy bear. She was white-faced but berry-mouthed and her hair was crimson-tipped and clogged with sweat. Clive stared at her, revolted.

'Eliot? Eliot?' Martha was crouched on the floor, holding Eliot by the shoulders and speaking into her face.

'Do we need an ambulance?' Tom asked in a blanched voice.

Martha did not answer him, and Clive was speechless.

Now Eliot moaned, hinged and scratched up a dry heave. Then she spoke: 'Oh God I feel so bad.' It came out in a sea-gull's mewl.

'Are you going to be sick again?' Martha asked her.

'It hurts it hurts,' Eliot wailed, 'oh God –' She leaned over and gagged, but nothing came up. The breath rattled in her throat.

Clive said, 'What shall I do?'

'Call room service,' said Martha. 'Get that waiter up here.' She wetted a towel and wiped Eliot's face and hands. 'Eliot?' she said. 'Don't worry: you're going to be all right.' Eliot clutched at Martha's arms and started crying and gulping. Martha put an arm around her shoulders and a palm against her sweating, grey forehead.

The waiter arrived and gave Clive a long, cool look before

16

turning to Martha and Eliot, crouched in their heap on the floor. Martha – in her pants and damp, stained vest – turned her face up to him. Clive could see her breasts, her bare thighs and her knickers and he knew the waiter would be looking too; he wished she had been wearing more clothes, or wearing these clothes differently. Somehow the sweat and the smell – and even the ragged, fluttering seagull on the floor beside her – only increased her attraction.

Martha spoke in rapid, fluent French and the waiter nodded and frowned. Stepping into the bathroom he turned on the shower and soaked a hand towel in the basin. Then he crouched and, with Martha's help, hauled Eliot into the bathroom. The door was closed behind them.

Tom and Clive were shut out but they continued to stand where they were and listen to a conversation they could not comprehend. For ten minutes they heard intermittent discussion, occasional retching and the patter and hiss of the shower. Then the bathroom door opened and the waiter emerged, holding Eliot under the arms as if he were ejecting a local drunk from the bar downstairs. He tugged her into Clive and Martha's bedroom and slung her on to their bed. Martha perched next to her and the waiter fetched a blanket from the cupboard and tucked it round them both. Eliot, now exhausted, was forced by Martha to stay awake and take continual sips of water. Tom – desperate to do something – fetched his Discman and gave them a headphone each, asking, 'William Orbit or Leonard Cohen?'

Eliot's complexion had now settled to a waxy pallor – 'You actually look quite cool,' encouraged Tom, 'like a zombie.'

17

Martha's tanned skin, by comparison, looked as tempting and restorative as a jar of honey. The waiter certainly thought so – Clive saw his fingers brush her bare shoulders as he arranged the blanket.

'My throat hurts,' complained Eliot.

'It's all the puke,' said Tom. 'No smoking for a day or so, Chuffy.' He was so relieved he shivered with a kind of hysteria.

'Please,' whimpered Eliot, leaning into Martha's shoulder, 'I'll never smoke or drink again so help me God.'

A chambermaid appeared, at first curious and then dismissive, and dealt with the mess of the neighbouring room. Clive handed the waiter every remaining note he had. Still not a word had passed between them. Clive knew he had been blamed and that he could not have defended himself in any language: it had been he who had ordered '*les enfants*' – as he heard the waiter describe Eliot and Tom – their wine.

For the rest of the week the secret united Martha and Clive, and so did a new sense of responsibility. Tom begged his brother, 'You won't tell, will you?'

Clive hesitated – here was power – but Martha broke in, saying, 'No, he won't.'

The distance between the elder and the younger two grew again: Tom and Eliot were children; Clive and Martha adults. Clive had got his wish – but there was a spoiler: Eliot decided that she owed her life to Martha and began to worship her. While Martha bathed she sat on the lid of the loo and painted her nails. When Martha ate, Eliot ordered the same. A hundred times a day Eliot asked Martha, 'Is it "*le*" or "*la*"?' In the evenings they swam together alone, their heads bobbing in the water for what seemed to Clive like hours: talking, talking, always talking – no doubt, he fretted, about sex and men in general, and himself and Tom in particular.

Somewhat to Clive's surprise his relationship with Martha survived the incident and the holiday. He judged that the trip must have been, overall, a success when she reached for his hand beside the luggage carousel. 'Come to my house,' she said. 'Don't go back to College.' So Clive abandoned his single room on the Quad for Martha's grubby, shared house in the Cowley Road.

All this was good – it was far more and better than he had expected – but Clive recognised that their roles were as set, now, as if they had been married for a decade. The period of settling-in was over and he would play supplicant to Martha's mighty goddess for as long as they were together. He had learned that as long as he loved Martha his happiness would only be a tributary of hers; she would be the only source of his contentment. He waited at her hand and foot on bended knee. If she wanted to see him he was summoned, but if she did not she would tell him to leave her alone. 'You're getting on my nerves,' she might say, almost teasing but not quite. 'Come back tomorrow, when I've begun to miss you.' Clive was at the mercy of these savage instructions. He could see that it demeaned him to obey, but he saw no other way to keep her.

2

Finals blotted the landscape. Clive knew he would not excel – he did not have the ability – but his mother would not believe him. 'You might get a First,' she said. 'You never know.'

'No, Mum,' said Clive, 'I do know: I won't.'

'You might,' she soothed. 'Don't put yourself down.'

He snapped at her, 'Mum! Leave it, will you?'

'I'm just—'

'Forget it!'

Martha was expected to get a First. 'Bloody expectations,' she grumbled. 'The bane of my life.' Her father, she said, would be satisfied with nothing less. 'It's either that or my dead body.'

Clive met Martha's father only once, but it seemed enough to satisfy all parties. On their way to his cottage – a perfect May morning – Martha said, 'You know he's a writer, don't you?' She was nervous, which was unusual, and she seemed keen to signal to Clive that his occupation would explain or forgive what lay ahead.

'I read that book about the raven,' lied Clive. 'It was great.'

As they drove up to the little house, Clive could see Aiden Doyle sitting on a stone bench beside the front door. They parked the car – borrowed from Martha's housemate Viv – and walked right up to his feet before he stirred. 'I suppose I should get up,' he said in a well-furred voice.

'Don't be silly, Dad,' said Martha, bending to kiss him. 'This is Clive.'

'Hello, son.'

Aiden put down his glass to shake hands, and Clive realised that when Martha had said 'writer' she had meant 'drinker'. He felt a weariness spread through his limbs and a certainty that the day would not – could not – be a success.

Martha opened more wine and they sat outside on the bench in a row. 'PPE?' Aiden asked Clive. 'Something to do with gymnastics?' He snickered, scrabbling for a match from the box on his knee.

'Dad, don't be a tit,' Martha said. 'Clive's going to be a barrister.'

'Criminal?'

'Commercial,' answered Clive.

'Ah,' sneered Aiden. 'Your bank manager will very proud.'

It was a long day, and at the end of it Martha was quiet. As they drove back into Oxford she suggested, 'Shall I drop you

21

off?' Clive's heart sank: if she did not want him at her house tonight, he must have failed.

Alone that night and all the next day Clive trod water, waiting to be told he was dumped. The next evening Martha came to see him in his room. She pulled him down to sit beside her on his single bed. 'I'm sorry about my father,' she said. 'He was a pig to you. He's protective, that's all.'

Possessive, thought Clive, *not protective*. He was touched, however, and aloud he said, 'That's all right.'

Martha fiddled with his fingers in her own. Clive loved it when she did this – it was as if she had muddled them together and forgotten whose were whose; as if she cared as much for his as for her own. He braced himself. The thought of losing her almost made him choke. 'Clive,' she said, 'you know I love you, don't you?' She had not said it before. Clive held his breath. 'I love you,' she went on, 'because you're everything my dad's not. You're kind and good, and you look after me.' She turned her head to look at him – shy, for once – and he thought he might collapse, he loved her so much.

One Saturday they were surprised at home by a ring at the doorbell. Clive found Eliot on the doorstep. 'Fuck it's cold,' she said, stepping over the tiled porch floor, 'and I've walked miles. Any chance of a cuppa?'

She was on a school trip but had ditched the Ashmolean and come to visit, dressed in the army jacket, a pair of leggings and laced, black boots. 'It's my new look,' she said. 'It's kind of Patti Hearst minus the machine gun meets Patti Smith minus the microphone.' The gold bee clung to her lapel.

Neither Clive nor Martha wanted to entertain her. They shut her in the kitchen like an untrained puppy whilst they held a consultation outside.

'I've got so much work to do,' said Martha, panicking. 'I can't be distracted.'

'Don't worry,' soothed Clive. 'I'll take her out for a pizza or something.'

Eliot ate a packet of Monster Munch, pulling it from one of her jacket pockets, and made herself a Nescafé. 'You're so lucky,' she said. 'School is prison. I can't wait 'til I'm a student.'

She had been expelled from Tom's London school and sent to board in the country. *Eliot's know-all attitude*, her head teacher had written in the letter of expulsion, *does not augur well for a happy future.*

'Stupid cow,' was Eliot's comment. 'I bet she had to look up "augur" in the dictionary.'

The new school was 'dull as shit. Apart from music. If it wasn't for that I'd run away and marry a millionaire.' She was coarse and foul-mouthed, and Martha was getting irritated.

Clive intervened. 'Look: Martha wants to work – shall we go and get a cup of tea?'

'Fuck that,' Eliot said, grabbing his wrist to look at his watch. 'Let's go to the pub.'

Already the pub's interior was clouded by a haze of blue cigarette smoke which hung at eye level in the weak morning light. 'What'll it be?' said the landlord to Clive. The place still smelled of last night: stale beer and stale ashtrays, not freshened yet by today's spilled pints and stubbed-out fags.

Eliot pulled herself on to a stool. 'I'll have a Coke first,' she said, 'and then a Bloody Mary.'

'You're not eighteen, young lady,' said the landlord. 'So you can stick with a Coke.'

Eliot blinked, opened her mouth and shut it again. 'And a packet of dry-roasted peanuts,' she said in a small voice.

They carried their drinks to a corner table. 'That was so embarrassing,' said Eliot. 'I never normally get stopped.' She took a pack of Marlboro from a pocket and lit one.

'One day you'll be glad to look your age and not three years older,' said Clive.

'One day, maybe,' said Eliot, 'but not today. Anyway, I'm nearly sixteen – my birthday's next month. I'm going to have a party. Will you come? I'm going to invite Mr Lennox, my old teacher, and get him to dee-vee me. I'm not at the same school now, so he won't get the sack.'

'How considerate of you,' said Clive.

'I'm a nice girl,' she said. 'Anyway, when did you lose your virginity? Were you drunk? Was it a one-night stand? Was she some gopping minger covered in zits?'

'Shut up,' flushed Clive. 'It's none of your business.'

But Eliot was not listening. 'Oh my *God*,' she said. A peanut fell from her mouth on to the table.

'What?'

'The most good-looking man I've ever seen in my life has just walked in,' she said.

Clive followed her stare. '*That* man?' he said. 'I know him.'

It was Danny, an old boyfriend of Martha's whose existence haunted Clive. 'It was just a sex thing,' Martha had said of him.

'A lot of fun, but not exactly a meeting of the minds.' Nothing could have made Clive feel worse. *Just a sex thing.* Viv had also slept with Danny and described him as 'the best shag of my life.' Clive did not know what this meant – big cock? Unlimited stamina? The guaranteed delivery of multiple orgasms? – but he did not like the sound of it. Both women had agreed, 'He's a total bastard,' which meant no more or less than irresistible as far as Clive could tell. He feared and hated Danny, and dreaded a chance meeting.

Now Eliot pestered him: 'Can you say hello? Can we go and sit with him? Can you get him over here?'

Clive was about to say 'No!' and suggest they went somewhere else when Danny came over. 'Don't I know you?' he asked Clive. 'Aren't you a friend of Martha's?'

'I'm her boyfriend. I'm Clive.'

'Right. Listen – can I pinch a fag?'

'Yes, of course,' said Eliot. 'They're mine.' She pushed the pack towards him. 'I'm Eliot.'

'Thanks,' said Danny, taking one and lighting it. 'I only came in for a quick half and a slash – I'm on my way to the races.'

'Races?' said Eliot.

'Yeah, it's a local thing – a point-to-point.'

'Can we come?' asked Eliot.

Clive shot her a look but she ignored him.

Danny pondered them both and blew smoke through his nostrils. 'Sure,' he said, 'if you like. Just let me go and have a wazz.'

He disappeared into the Gents.

'Don't you have to be back at school?' Clive said to Eliot.

'Not 'til seven,' she said. 'I can get the bus. Come *on*, let's have some fun. If you don't want to come I'll go on my own.'

This was enough to persuade him. 'All right,' Clive said, 'we'll go.'

Danny climbed into a large, dirty Mercedes which was parked outside the pub. Eliot slid across the leather back seats. 'This car is fucking cool,' she said. Every 'fuck' startled Clive like the sudden bark of a dog.

'It's not mine,' said Danny. 'It belongs to a woman who owes me money.'

Eliot picked up a stack of sports pages from the seat next to her and asked, 'Are you a bookie?'

'Sort of,' said Danny. 'Sometimes.'

'But I thought you were a student?' said Clive.

Danny laughed. 'Student? No, mate. Didn't see the point.'

They stopped for fuel, Coke and cigarettes before Danny headed south-west towards the high, pale crease of the chalk downs. It was a raw day to be outdoors: the approaching hills looked cold and bare and a torn, white sky scudded behind them. The hedges beside the road were black and glittering after a long night's rain.

Eliot rummaged through a box of cassettes next to her in the back. 'I like your music.'

'Pass me something and I'll put it on.'

She was struck by a sudden shyness. 'Oh,' she said, 'no – it's OK.'

There was something already between them – a current; a recognition – that Clive did not feel party to. Without Martha he had lost his mooring; he did not know where to put himself, or what sort of person to be. He felt a cold key turn in his guts, and he wished they had not come.

Danny turned from one road to another, each more slender than the last, following yellow-painted signs that stuck out from the hedges and read, 'Race Meeting'. A sloshing, puddled lane led them into a greasy field where the heavy Mercedes glided to a stop. 'We'll never get out,' said Eliot cheerfully. 'It's a swamp.'

A white-faced crowd stood hunched against the blast of wind and ice-splintered rain. Two tents – one labelled 'Beer' and the other, 'Food' – billowed and guttered on their ropes. Children with mottled, marbled faces were galloping through the chalky paste, skidding and jumping to keep warm. Dogs trembled at the end of their leads, hovering above the turf as if they could not bear to stand or sit.

Clive stared through the car window. He yearned for the fug of Martha's bedroom: the flickering blade of the gas flame; the smell of her Golden Virginia; tea going cold in the mug and a stilted trickle of condensation puddling on the window sill.

'I'm going to freeze my tits off,' Eliot said.

Danny was unfazed. 'Not if you drink enough,' he said. 'Guinness and whisky—'

'Yum.'

'—and there are coats in the back.'

They got out of the car – even Clive swore when the wind

hit him – and Danny pulled a long, dark-checked cashmere overcoat from the boot. 'This looks expensive,' he said. He handed it to Eliot.

She put it on, knotted the belt and said, 'Holy crap, this is gorgeous. I'm never taking it off.'

Clive turned to look and saw a person quite altered: dressed in a woman's coat, Eliot had borrowed a woman's glamour. Danny lifted his head from the boot and looked her over. 'Wow,' he said, and Eliot glowed.

Clive felt a pinch in his heart. 'Anything for me?' he asked. Danny passed him a green cagoule and a pair of rubber boots and Clive dithered, dismayed. He wanted to be warm but not to look ridiculous. He shrugged his way into the anorak and looked down at himself.

Eliot saw him and laughed. 'Jeremy Fisher,' she said, her wicked little head cocked to one side.

Clive blushed and tried to think of a reply but Eliot had already turned away, trotting alongside Danny towards the beer tent. Clive slid and floundered behind them. *Jeremy Fisher.* He smarted.

The marquee was stifling and clammy and roared with noise. Everyone seemed to be drunk and laughing. Eliot looked around, delighted. 'This is going to be fun,' she said, but Danny was steered away by welcoming arms and without him she seemed to deflate. 'I'm hungry,' she whined, 'and I want a drink. Will you buy me one?' They pushed their way to the bar. Eliot whispered, 'Why am I getting funny looks?'

'Because you look like an anti.' It was Danny, appearing beside them.

'Do I?' Eliot looked down at herself. 'Anti what?'

Danny laughed. 'Come on, get the drinks in and we'll go outside for the first race.'

Clive ordered three pints of Guinness and three whiskies and they swallowed them in that order. Eliot went pink and cross-eyed. 'Shall we put some money on?' she asked Danny.

'Put a tenner on Mr Bricks if you like – but don't go blaming me if he doesn't win.'

'Clive, have you got another tenner?'

'It's my last one.'

'I bet it's not – you're always loaded.'

'Not loaded. Careful.'

'Not around me you're not,' she jeered. 'Come on – don't be such a tight-arse.' She followed Danny out into the wind.

Clive placed the bet and joined them by the finishing post. Danny was standing behind Eliot and had wrapped both arms around her to keep her warm; her heels rested on the toes of his boots and she was leaning back against him, laughing.

Looking at them Clive felt a stab of pain that surprised him. He turned away to recover himself, before it showed on his face. These feelings were alarming; he did not want to name them. He was confused. He would have felt better with Martha here but nevertheless he was glad she was not. A mass of people stood and jostled him and he thought he might be trampled underfoot or lost like the frantic dog which trailed a scarlet lead and scanned the crowd, over and over, with worried eyes and a dipping, searching nose.

The noise was non-stop: talking, laughing, calling and shouting that grew to a chorus and then to a blurring, beating roar as the race began. Behind it the commentary fogged out of the loudspeaker but Clive could make neither head nor tail of it – how could anyone? It was deafening but incomprehensible – and nor could he see anything but heads, legs and mud.

'Come on, Mr Bricks!' shouted Eliot. 'Get a fucking move on!'

A tidy couple beside them turned at her voice with eyebrows raised and Danny said, 'Sorry,' to them and then added, 'I can't take her anywhere,' and squeezed Eliot until she yelped and wriggled in his grasp, wild with whisky and excitement. Clive, watching, felt a throb of anger. *She is not yours*, he thought. But whose?

The pulse of the crowd became more thunderous still. 'Christ alive,' said Danny, leaning forward, 'he's going to do it.'

He did not shout, but Eliot did: 'Come on! Come on!'

Clive could not seem to raise his voice; he could not bear to hear his feeble bleat amid that dreadful roar. All around them people yelled, cursed, stamped and shook their fists and then in a gasp and a blur the two leading horses ground past the post, filthy and exhausted. At once the noise became an indeterminate groan of relief or disappointment. Eliot turned to Clive. 'How much did you put on?'

'That tenner I had.'

'Only ten quid? Fuck! We could have minted it. What have we won?'

'What did you get? Nine to one? Something like that?' Danny quizzed him.

'Something like that,' lied Clive. It had been more like seven.

'Well, that's not bad,' said Eliot, rolling her eyes to the sky as she did the maths in her head. 'Plenty for cakes and ale!' She snatched the betting slip from Clive's hand. 'Come on, Pops,' she said, 'let's go and fetch our winnings.'

But neither money nor beer could bring Clive back from where he teetered, at the edge of a blind rage. He sensed Danny and Eliot pulling away from him as if they had climbed into a little two-seater and left him standing at the kerb.

'Why are you in such a grump?' Eliot asked him, back in the tent with more drinks.

'Because I should be working,' said Clive in a sulky voice. 'I can't just piss about.'

'Piss about?' said Danny. 'This is my office. I've made a killing today – you've brought me luck.' He ruffled Eliot's hair and kissed her hot cheek.

She blushed and stammered, 'Have I?'

Clive had had enough – he wanted Eliot's joyous, laughing attention turned to him and if he could not have it, he wanted to go home. Now she was trying to pick a horse to back in the next race: 'Some of these names are hilarious,' she said. 'What about Miss Demeanour? That's got to be worth a fiver.'

'You're what my nan would call "a caution",' commented Danny.

'Or, Frankly Marvellous? That's a good one for you. Hey, here's one for Clive,' she went on. 'Rigger Tony. Geddit? *Rigatoni.* Isn't that a kind of pasta?' She turned to Danny. 'Clive's real name is Tony but he hated it so he swapped.'

'Swapped it for Clive?' They both looked him over.

This was not the attention Clive had wanted. 'No one calls me Tony anymore,' he said.

'My dad was called Tony,' said Danny. 'He's dead now.'

'That's shitty,' sympathised Eliot. 'I had a brother who died when I was a baby.'

In the silence that followed, Clive, with dark fury, considered his family: alive and well, and at home in Amersham. Peter would be in the garden, Val in the kitchen and Tom in his bedroom with the music on loud. They would eat a homemade curry later and then Tom would say, 'I'm going out,' and his mother would try to stop him. 'Must you?' she would say. 'It's so cold. Don't you want to stay and watch a film with us?' Tom would kiss her and go, nonetheless.

'Amersham is so convenient,' Val always said. 'It's only forty minutes to John Lewis on Oxford Street.'

This comment irritated Clive every time he heard it. 'Mum, it's not. It's an hour to Baker Street, and then you have to change to the Bakerloo line, and there's the taxi from here to the station, *and* back again in the evening. It all mounts up.'

But his mother would play deaf, look away, and not respond.

Clive had never heard before about Eliot's dead brother – he wondered if she were even telling the truth. She was a climbing weed that twisted round them, rootless and threading, a clinging twine. She would attach herself to anyone. She had been Tom's – Martha's – his parents' – and then this morning –

for a moment only – she had been his, but now she was Danny's. Danny had eclipsed them all.

'My dad was a bastard,' he was saying. 'I was glad when he died.'

'My mum's a cow,' commiserated Eliot.

Clive was sick of the pair of them. 'I want to go,' he said. 'I'm cold.'

'You should drink more,' said Eliot.

'No – you should drink less.' He hated himself but he could not resist: 'I don't fancy cleaning up your mess again.'

Eliot flushed and said nothing.

'You can both relax,' said Danny. 'No one's going anywhere until I'm done.'

'I like your job,' said Eliot. 'I'm going to be a concert pianist when I grow up, and Clive's going to be a barrister.'

'I'm grown-up already,' spluttered Clive.

'A barrister?' said Danny. 'That's good – I can come to you when I get done for illegal gambling.'

Eliot giggled. 'And I can come to you when I divorce my first millionaire.'

They both laughed.

'No you can't,' said Clive. 'You'll need a solicitor – and anyway, it's a different kind of law.'

At last they were back in the car and Danny turned the heater to full blast. 'Where's school?' he asked Eliot.

'Ugh,' she said, tipping her head back on to the headrest. 'The other side of Swindon. Why?'

'Because we might as well drop you off.'

'Shit, that would be amazing,' said Eliot. 'I was just thinking how much I didn't want to sit on that frigging bus.'

Eliot had got into the front – 'Come on, Clive, be fair, you were in the front on the way' – and Clive the back. He was the toddler strapped into its seat; the dog kept behind a grille; the spare wheel in the boot. He stared at the backs of their heads and hated them.

On the road again, Danny switched on the radio and a piano concerto poured out like a torrent of water.

'Can we have this?' asked Eliot. 'It's Brahms.'

Danny turned it up. 'Brahms what?' he asked, impressed.

'Second piano concerto,' said Eliot. She tugged at her earlobe, self-conscious. 'Not just a pretty face, you see,' she joked.

Clive could not bear it: 'Proper little madam, aren't you?' he said, 'with your hockey stick and your piano lessons.'

Eliot said nothing, and Danny reached forward and turned up the radio's volume.

They drove in silence until Eliot cleared her throat and said, 'It's the next right turn.' Pulling in between wrought-iron gates the headlights swept over what looked like miles of parkland.

'Blimey,' said Danny. 'Can I stay too?'

Eliot giggled. 'Only if you wear a skirt – no boys allowed.'

'I could teach you sums.'

'I wish,' sighed Eliot. She pointed into the dark and said, 'Hockey pitches, tennis courts, running track. That's the science department' – they passed a jumble of modern buildings –

'and that's the headmistress's house.' As they drew alongside a stolid little bungalow she added, 'The stupid turd.'

At the end of a slick, black drive the car scrunched on to a lake of gravel. Danny pulled up in front of the house: a vast, sand-coloured building which sheltered behind six towering columns. A flight of stone steps led up to the front door and on either side of the bottom stair lay a stone lion with crossed front paws and a 'Have you been drinking?' expression.

'For Christ's sake,' Danny said, putting the car into 'Park', 'it's a bloody palace.' They all three sat in contemplative silence for a moment. Then Danny turned to face Eliot and asked, 'Will you be all right?'

'Yes of course,' she said. 'And thank you for a lovely day.' It was a different voice from the one which had demanded beer and cigarettes, and it sounded much younger. As she fiddled with the door handle Clive saw that she was trying not to cry.

'That's all right, pet,' said Danny. 'It was fun, wasn't it?'

Eliot nodded.

'Here, you'd better take some fags,' said Danny. He handed her the pack from his pocket. 'And what else? Have a look in the glove box.'

Eliot clicked open the glove compartment and pulled out a Twix bar. 'Can I take this *and* the fags?' she asked, sounding happier. 'I'll pay you back.'

Danny laughed. 'Yes, you can.'

Clutching her presents Eliot turned in her seat. ''Bye, Clive,' she said. 'See you in London. Come to my birthday, will you? Both of you? It's in a month.' She opened the door and got out. Then she said, 'Oh shit, the coat,' and started to take it off.

'Keep it,' said Danny. 'It suits you.'

'Really?' Eliot was ecstatic. 'Thanks.' She put the cigarettes and the chocolate in her pocket and tied the belt tightly around herself.

'Hang on,' said Clive to Danny, 'I'm going to get in the front.' He got out of the car and tried to grab Eliot's elbow as she turned away. ''Bye, Eliot,' he said. He had thought he might hug her but she had stepped just out of reach and was walking away from him, turning up the collar on her wonderful coat.

She sang out a loose 'Goodbye' over her shoulder.

Clive watched her go up the steps, two by two, until Danny said, 'Get in, will you? It's too bloody cold to hang about.'

Martha lifted her head and laughed when Clive told her they had been asked to Eliot's birthday party. 'How sweet,' she said, poised above her revision.

'Do you want to go?'

'Go? Are you mad? I'm trying to get a First, Clive, not a degree in being a teenage dropout.'

'It's Primrose Hill. Isn't that your neck of the woods? Where your dad used to live?'

Martha gave a snort. 'Believe me, Primrose Hill is a long way from Kilburn.'

Part II

3

Did he remember Eliot Fox? In his London bedroom Clive folded his suit trousers neatly in half at the waist so that he could press the two legs together and smooth them over a wooden coat hanger which hung from a hook on the back of the bedroom door. He had left the jacket in the kitchen, slung over the back of a chair, and he wondered whether or not to retrieve it. What a lot of effort it all was.

He stood in his shirt, pants and socks and looked up at the trousers on their hanger until Martha said, 'Earth to Clive?' and he turned to see her watching him, amused, wiping one eyelid with a cotton-wool ball.

'Sorry,' he said. 'I was just trying to remember. She was Tom's friend, right?'

'Yes! God!' said Martha. She turned away again with her attention on the other eye. 'I thought you'd be more interested – I can remember everything about her: she came to

France, Tom was in love with her (but of course they were only about fifteen so it wasn't really *love*-love) and then she got the hots for Danny – remember him? – and Tom nearly went demented.'

'That's right,' said Clive. His voice sounded as pale as he imagined his face to be. 'Now I remember.' But what to do about the jacket? He would leave it where it was, he decided. What harm could it come to in the kitchen overnight?

'Oh' – now Martha was rubbing cream into her hands – 'and there's some other news, deadly dull: there are bats, having babies in the cottage roof. It's called a maternity colony – there are hundreds of the little buggers. Steve found them, looking for the leak. He says they're protected and he can't fix anything up there 'til they've gone.'

The next morning Clive ran all the way to his office in Chambers.

This was something he did once a week and considered quite normal, but it seemed to make other people as angry and defensive as if he had told them he was religious, or teetotal. 'All the way to Chancery Lane?' they would comment, gaping at him. 'Are you *mad*? That's *miles*.'

'About five-and-a-half miles, if you go in a straight line,' Clive would say.

This morning, after he had changed and drunk a lot of water from the cooler, he walked into his colleague Belinda's office. 'Have you got a minute?' he asked, and shut the door. He was no longer out of breath, but his heart beat very fast. 'It's Eliot Fox,' he began.

It was only seven a.m. and Belinda's face was still cross-hatched with sleep. While he explained – 'London – piano – Eliza' – she took off her glasses and rubbed at her eyes, and when he had finished she put the glasses back on and blinked up at him.

'Jesus,' she said. 'It's your worst nightmare.'

Clive had already had the same thought, but when he heard it spoken aloud he flinched.

Belinda did not believe in coffee shops but she did believe in kettles, mugs and instant coffee. Clive watched the sugar dissolve from his teaspoon.

'There are two ways you can play it,' said Belinda. 'The first is total denial. The wall.'

'Or?'

'Come clean.'

Come clean, thought Clive. He pictured himself on his knees with a scrubbing brush. It would be no use; those stains were indelible. 'How?' he asked.

'What do you mean, "how"? *Come clean*. Clean as a whistle: tell Martha everything.'

Piano lessons lasted forty-five minutes but, 'For the last five,' said Miss Fox, 'we'll listen to a bit of something. We only have this term together so we might as well enjoy ourselves.'

Eliza was not used to enjoying herself, and certainly not at school. She did not trust her luck: her lessons so far with Miss Fox had seemed too good to be true, so it was typical that they would only go on for one term. Her proper teacher,

Mrs Bridges, had gone off to have a baby – probably in a maternity colony, like one of the bats that Eliza and her mother had looked up on the computer – and Miss Fox was the substitute.

'You look too nice for a real teacher,' Eliza told her.

Miss Fox smiled. 'That's a relief,' she said.

Eliza had been given a biscuit to nibble as she listened to Miss Fox play the piano for the last five minutes of the lesson. Lessons with Mrs Bridges had not included biscuits, and even if they had the biscuits would not have been like this one. It was brittle and Italian, and contained pieces of almond. Eliza was not certain she liked it, but she knew it must be delicious and special because it came from Miss Fox. Pleasing her new teacher was all that she wanted to do, now and always, and so she wrapped her legs around the legs of the piano stool and thought of something nice to say when Miss Fox next paused in her playing.

The first thing that came into her head was, 'I like your hair,' which also happened to be true.

'I like yours,' Miss Fox responded.

Now Eliza fingered the end of her ponytail, speechless with pleasure.

'What about this?' Miss Fox played a bit of something solemn. 'Do you like that?'

Eliza wrinkled her nose. 'It sounds like maths. Have you got a husband?' she asked quickly before Miss Fox began to play again. 'Or children?'

'No. Have you got brothers or sisters?'

'No. Mum dropped me down the stairs by accident when I was little, so she didn't want any more babies after that.'

Miss Fox looked at her in the way that people tended to do when Eliza delivered this information. Eliza quite enjoyed the effect; Martha, if she overheard her daughter, did not.

'I was all right,' Eliza reassured her teacher, 'but Mum was really upset for ages.'

'Yes,' said Miss Fox, 'I expect she was.'

'It was all her fault, you see – she was supposed to be looking after me. I had to go and live in intensive care, in the hospital. I don't remember it but Dad does and so does Mum but she doesn't like to talk about it.'

There was no response to this.

'Dad says I'm the only child that ever got cleverer after falling on its head,' Eliza said, kicking the legs of the piano stool.

'That's right – you come top in everything, don't you?'

Eliza made a face. 'Not swimming,' she said. 'And coming top is kind of good and kind of bad. Mum, Dad and the teachers like me but everyone else hates my guts. It's not good to know stuff, at school. Or do stuff.'

Miss Fox did not try to argue or sympathise but instead played something else. 'What about that – does that sound like maths?'

'No,' said Eliza, 'that sounds nice – what is it?'

'They were both Bach,' replied Miss Fox. 'From something called *The Well-Tempered Clavier*. It's my favourite piece of music.'

'It's a nice-sounding name,' said Eliza, thinking it over. 'What's a "clavier"?'

'It's another word for a piano – an old-fashioned one. "Well-tempered" actually means "tuned".'

'It sounds like the piano's in a very good mood,' said Eliza. Just then the bell rang in the corridor outside. 'Yuck,' she added. 'Now it really *is* maths.'

When Clive came home from work there was a bicycle chained to the railings outside the house. He stood and looked at it for a moment, suspicious and afraid.

If Belinda had been there she would have said, 'You are insufficiently prepared for this meeting. Walk away. Pretend you got stuck at work. Come back when she is gone.'

Clive told his feet to take him away, but instead – *traitors!* – they took him up the steps to the front door and through it, into the communal hall where he was faced with a brimming tide of junk mail that tried to lap back over the threshold and into the open air. He waded through the leaflets and cellophane envelopes to the door of his flat, turned his key in the lock and pushed the door open an inch. *This is my home, and now Eliot Fox is in it.*

Hearing voices and laughter he opened the gap a little wider. He cocked his head and listened to Martha's low murmur and Eliza's shrill interruption, 'No, *no*, Mum – it's not there, I've already looked.' It sounded ordinary and harmless. Perhaps he had been mistaken; perhaps the bike was innocent. Encouraged, Clive walked forward into the flat.

The hallway was tight and small with hung-up coats and he imagined hiding (in a pocket, or folded into a pair of winter gloves, or tucked into Eliza's woolly hat and bundled on to a shelf) until the threat of Eliot Fox had passed, but again his feet took him forward. At the threshold of the next room – the kitchen – he teetered, holding his breath and wondering – *Is she here or is she not?* – and then there was a movement – the glimpse of a movement – in one corner. He turned his head.

The room was dim after the sunlit throb of the street. Clive could make out only a shape: something – someone – facing him with folded arms and a sharp silhouette. There was really nothing of her – just a narrow blade, resting on its point – and yet Eliot seemed to occupy the room, to take up more space than she ought and to leave him no air for himself.

She was alone. Martha and Eliza were downstairs. Now Clive felt short of breath.

The kettle came to a furious, rummaging boil and switched itself off. Into the silence Clive cowered and flinched before he spoke: 'Eliot?' He peered at the shape of her, not trusting his vision.

She did not reply at once and there was a moment of suspension as if his words were travelling to her through the air in slow motion. But then in a quiet, cool voice she said, 'I bet you wish you'd told her, Clive. What are we going to do now?'

Clive put out straying fingertips to steady himself on the back of a chair. He opened his mouth but whether to breathe or speak he did not know. He pictured himself turning over as he fell through the air from a great height – this was a dream he had had so many times before, for so many years, and he knew how it would be: it always ended just before he hit the ground and today – here – now – awake and before he could speak—

'Dad! Dad! Dad! Mum! It's Dad!'

—Eliza had run up the stairs and into the room to grab him by the hand.

45

4

Eliot had come back to the house from the school gates, pushing her bike alongside Martha and Eliza on the pavement.

'You'll come in, won't you?' Martha had said. 'Just for a moment?'

'Please?' Eliza had begged, hopping between them over the cracks.

It was plain that Eliza had fallen in love with Miss Fox. 'I know I shouldn't mind,' Martha confessed to Clive in private, 'but I do.'

I do too, Clive thought.

'It won't last,' he said aloud, in a level, careless voice. 'It's a crush.'

'They're the worst!' laughed Martha. 'Crushes are dangerous – you've no idea what little girls are like.'

*

Clive pictured Eliza leading Eliot round his home:

'– This is the hall, this is the kitchen, this is where we watch TV and down here are the bedrooms, come and look, this is Mum and Dad's and this is mine, it's really small –'

This was Eliot, pulled by the hand from room to room: Eliot looking, Eliot standing, Eliot peering and Eliot seeing.

At last she said, 'I ought to go,' and they all went out to the step.

Eliza was hot-headed with excitement and attention. 'It's so weird,' she said, 'isn't it, Dad? That Miss Fox is my teacher? And you're all friends?'

But Clive was fiddling with the catch on the door and didn't hear her.

Martha laughed and took Eliza's hand. 'Life before you, Eliza – can you imagine?' She was teasing and happy.

Clive followed Eliot down to her bike. With his back to the house he took a breath and asked her quietly, 'Are you going to tell?'

It shocked him to hear his own voice, speaking that question aloud. Eliot, however, did not seem surprised. She unlocked two locks and steadied the bike against her hip while she slid the keys into a pocket. Her reply – quiet; half-smiling – mystified him: 'Tell Martha? I won't have to.'

She looked over his shoulder to wave at his wife and daughter, smiling on the top step, and then she pedalled away.

*

'Well,' Martha said, back in the flat with the door shut. 'How about that? Eliot Fox, no less, in our house. What would Tom say? I can't wait to tell him. Or do you want to?'

But Clive was lost for words.

Later, sitting at the kitchen table with her homework Eliza said, 'Miss Fox says if we go to her house at the weekend I can practise. Can we?'

'Yes, of course,' said Martha. 'We'll go on Saturday.'

'Instead of swimming?' said Eliza, perking up.

'As well as swimming.'

'Bum. Dad too?'

Clive was staring at the computer screen. 'No,' he said. 'I have to work.'

Eliza cut her losses and subsided into her seat. She remained, however, distracted from her studies by her new favourite topic. 'Dad, don't you think Miss Fox is really cool?'

Clive said nothing.

Martha glanced at him. 'She was always cool,' she said, stepping in. 'Even aged fifteen. Tom was in love with her – did you know that?'

If Martha resented Eliza's love for Eliot, thought Clive, she didn't show it. She sounded as loving and admiring of Eliot as Eliza could wish her to be. *That is good parenting*, he thought. *Skilful lying.* He stared at the computer screen in front of him where words seemed to wash and shimmer from one side to the other like a flock of starlings.

'Uncle Tom? Miss Fox?' Eliza goggled. 'Fifteen?' Now her books did not interest her in the slightest. She stared out of the window, twisting her pen in her hair – something she did during moments of contemplation. 'It's funny – isn't it,' she said, 'that Miss Fox and I both have almost the same name. I mean the "E – l – i" part.'

'Yes,' said Martha, 'I thought that too. We might get you muddled up!'

This was a joke but it was a lovely idea; Eliza smiled with pleasure, twisting the pen. 'Isn't it funny, Dad?' she repeated.

'Hilarious,' said Clive. He used a flat, dead voice to smother the whole subject.

Martha and Eliza were muted and Clive cursed himself. *Pull yourself together.* Turning his head from the screen he said, 'I'm a bit . . . I think I'll go for a walk.'

Martha looked at him with a question mark on her face that expected an answer, but Eliza had knitted her pen into her hair and got it stuck.

'Ow,' she bleated, turning in her seat to face her mother. 'Help.'

'Ridiculous child!' said Martha. The two were locked together, unknotting and detangling, when Clive slid out of the door.

He stood on the step and wondered where to go. *Eliot Fox has got me out of my house,* he thought in surprise. *Already.* He felt a current of fear, as if a worm had been sleeping inside him and now it was awake, rippling its length along his guts.

Absurd! He shook his head at himself and trotted down the steps.

Each morning Belinda smoked one cigarette, standing on the bit of broken tarmac behind the office. 'My club room,' she called it. Belinda preferred pronouncements to conversation: 'I have to have one ciggie with my *caffè istante*. Otherwise I can't go to the loo and then the whole day falls apart.' No one could argue with this.

Today Clive followed her out of the emergency exit and told her what had happened. After puffing, sipping and coughing she said, 'I thought I told you not to see Eliot.'

'She was in my house!' Clive protested. 'What could I do?'

'Make something up. Leave. Go back later.'

'I can't start lying—'

'Start? What do you mean, *start*? You've been lying for *years*.'

'Well ...' began Clive. 'I never actually told any lies, not actual lies—'

'Oh, God,' she interrupted him. 'Men!' She was really angry; he took a step back. 'What bullshit you talk!' She mimicked the bleat of his voice: '"*Never lied, never lied*" – haven't you heard of lying by omission?'

'OK, OK.' Clive tried to placate her.

'I don't want to hear about this, Clive. I'm serious. I've told you before.'

'It's just that ... I don't know what to do.'

'Go away. Leave me alone. These are my favourite three minutes of the day, and you're spoiling them.'

Clive had known Belinda would not tell.

'I wish you hadn't told me any of that,' she had responded to his confession. 'It's a bad, rotten deed, what you did. If I were Martha and I found out –'

He had quaked to hear her judge him. He had wished he'd

held his tongue. He would have knelt at her feet and begged for her silence, if need be, but—

'The only thing that matters now is Eliza,' Belinda had told him. 'Let's not mention it again.'

—and Clive had been reprieved.

He had been safe, then, but he was not safe now.

Saturday afternoon began well. Martha and Eliza took three buses to Eliot's house which was a stout, brick villa at the top of a leafy hill.

'I like it round here,' said Eliza.

'I'm not surprised' – Martha was in buoyant mood – 'we're in Hampstead.'

Eliot opened the door in denim shirt and jeans.

'How do you manage to look so young?' Martha said. 'I said the same thing to Clive the other day. And you used to be so grown-up, for your age! It's not fair.'

It was a sincere – if glib – compliment, but Eliot did not enjoy it. 'I wasn't,' she frowned. 'I don't.'

Martha had said the wrong thing. How could it be? She had been rebuffed.

Then Eliot seemed to relent. 'It feels like a lifetime since those days.'

'It's more than my whole lifetime,' piped up Eliza. '*Years* more.'

Looking at the little girl, Eliot smiled. 'That's right.'

Once inside the hall – empty, echoing – Eliza said in surprise, 'But there's nothing here. Is this where you live?'

'Only just,' said Eliot. 'I lived in America until the other day.'

'Don't you have any stuff?'

'Just my piano. And a bed of course.' There was a pause. Eliza was expecting more and it came – at last – in small, rationed mouthfuls. 'This is my friend's house. He's selling it, but he's letting me stay for a bit.'

'Your friend must be massively rich,' Eliza sighed. 'Where has he moved to?'

'He's got lots of houses,' said Eliot. 'So he can choose from different places.'

'We've got two houses,' Eliza said – and then corrected herself: 'Well, sort of. A flat and a cottage.'

Martha blushed. 'Eliza, do stop—'

'And so have Stan and Jack.'

'—rabbiting on.' To Eliot, Martha explained, 'Stan and Jack are Eliza's cousins. Tom's twins.'

It was another mistake: the spoken name seemed to create a smashed silence, as if Martha had dropped a stack of plates. *But it was so many years ago*, she thought. *How can it still matter?*

Eliza had expected the piano to be a beautiful antique but it was a plain, black upright, scuffed at the corners. A pair of unpolished pedals poked out from underneath, like the slippers of a tired but obedient servant. It was a disappointment – but then Eliot stroked the lid with her palm before she opened it, as if she were greeting her favourite horse in its stable, and so Eliza knew that despite its appearance it must be special. She spelled in her head the plain, gold letters of its name: *C. Bechstein*. 'Is it old?' she asked, too shy to touch it.

'About a hundred years old,' said Eliot. 'So yes for a person, but no for a piano.' She adjusted the stool to suit Eliza's height. 'Half an hour,' she said, 'and then a break.'

'OK,' said Eliza, resigned. She began to pull her music from her rucksack and then said, 'I won't play 'til you go, Mum. You know I don't like you listening in.'

'I didn't like to play for my parents either,' Eliot said.

Eliza was pleased when she heard this, but Martha was hurt.

In the kitchen with Martha, Eliot opened the fridge door and asked, 'Will you have champagne? I found a whole case in a cupboard.'

'I like the sound of your friend,' said Martha. 'Yes please.' She was embarrassed when Eliot did not drink it herself. 'Won't you?' she said.

'No, I won't . . . I don't. Not anymore.'

She meant alcohol, and thinking of it Martha said, 'Do you remember France?'

'Yes.'

It was the end of both subjects: France and drinking.

Martha sipped her champagne. She wished she did not feel such a fool but why did she? She had expected laughter and stories but this reminded her of an interview.

They sat in the garden, a brick-flagged square the size of a ping-pong table and yet containing, somehow, two wooden chairs and a glossy magnolia tree. The high walls of the surrounding houses peered over them. 'Not much of a garden,' Eliot said.

Martha hinted, 'I suppose it depends what you're used to.' She wanted to know more about America.

Eliot, however, did not respond and in the end Martha had to fill the silence herself. 'You're lucky,' she said. 'I'd kill for some outside space.'

A magnolia leaf, bottle green and velvet brown, clattered through the branches to the ground. 'Odd how much noise they make,' Eliot said. 'Like falling slates.'

'I'd never noticed.' Martha felt disadvantaged, as if there would always be sights and sounds that reached Eliot's eyes and ears but not her own.

Clive worked on Saturdays – or at least, spent the mornings in his office – and then went to a smart, spacious gym where he swam or ran on the machine. Afterwards he would sit in the steam room and look down at his body, pleased. When it came to supper time – pizzas, on Saturdays – he could eat without guilt.

Today he would not get that opportunity. Changing back into his clothes he read a message on his phone: *Mum drunk can you come.*

He rang Martha's number. 'What does this mean?'

Martha's voice was thickened by alcohol: 'I think she wants you to join us. So do I. It's really nice here.'

'Are you drunk?' He knew she was – he could hear it in her voice – but he wanted to let her know that she had been caught.

'No! Of course not. I've only had ... a glass ... of champagne. Or so.'

'I can't come,' said Clive, thinking of what Belinda had said. 'It's impossible.'

But then it was Eliza's voice in his ear: 'You *have* to come. Miss Fox says we can all have pizzas here. She says there's a place around the corner, it's really good, they throw the whatsit – the dough – in the air. Come *on*, Dad.'

He could not say no.

When he arrived Eliza opened the door and tried to tug him into the house. 'Come on, Dad, we've all been waiting—'

'We're not staying,' he said to her, 'we're going. Now.'

She looked up at him. 'But—'

'Get your stuff. Where's Mum?'

'I'm here,' Martha stepped forward from the hall behind Eliza. 'What's the problem?' She spoke in a low voice. If they were going to have an argument she did not want it carrying to Eliot's sensitive ears.

'I want to go.'

'Well, I don't,' announced Eliza. 'You said yes to pizzas. You *said.*'

'No I didn't.'

'Why – are – you – such – a – P – I – G?' Eliza retreated – slow, meaningful steps on her sneakered feet – into the house.

This was mutiny. Clive somehow felt that if he stepped over the threshold all would be lost.

Martha leaned forward towards him and hissed, 'What the fuck is your problem?'

'You're drunk.'

'So? You're being a *dick*.'

Now Clive began to panic. 'Your breath smells of champagne,' he accused her, wrinkling his nose.

Martha laughed in his face.

Eliza shouted from the hall, 'Why do we have to go home? There's nothing at home. *Nothing.* We never do anything, we never go anywhere and you don't have any friends.'

Eliot stepped forward from the shadowed room. 'Hello, Clive,' she said. 'Do you want to get back? But listen –' she turned to Martha, 'Eliza doesn't have to go. She can stay with me, for pizza, if she wants. I can bring her back to you later.'

'Yes!' – this was Eliza, pirouetting on the bare floor.

'*No.*'

'Yes-yes-yes!'

'Why not? It's a good idea,' Martha said to her husband.

'I said, *no*, OK? We've got plans for the evening already, remember?'

This was not – quite – a lie, but nor was it a reason. Martha looked at him for a moment more but then she turned away and told Eliza to get her rucksack. 'Don't argue and stop showing off. Just do as you're told.'

Clive had won. He stood on the step and waited. Sunlight pressed the back of his head.

'We can have pizzas next time,' Eliot said to Eliza. 'And by the way: never mind "Miss Fox", OK? Call me Eliot. Miss Fox sounds so . . . *wicked*.' Her eyes sparkled as she smiled at Eliza.

*

The compliment of familiarity made Eliza's day; her mood was restored at once. She skipped along the street ahead of her parents.

'We're taking a taxi,' said Martha.

'There won't be one all the way out here,' countered Clive.

Martha stuck out her hand and, on cue, a black cab stopped beside it. Martha was triumphant. 'Serves you bloody well right for being such a toad,' she said. Her words seemed all to loll out together like an unrolling bandage – she must have drunk more than she thought. The air in the back of the cab seemed awfully close and she was sliding around on the seat as if it were the deck of a ship. Feeling suddenly sick, she opened the window.

'Don't do that,' snapped Clive. 'The air-conditioning is on.'

'I want fresh air,' said Martha, with an edge in her voice. 'Not conditioned air.'

Eliza was facing them from one of the jump seats and trying to make it flip up with her folded inside. They did not often take taxis – Martha was strict about public transport – so she was determined to make the most of the trip. 'This is going to be so expensive,' she said happily. 'It's *miles* to get home.' Her observation was greeted with silence. Looking from one parent to the other she saw two grim, set expressions; both faces turned to the window.

Arguments worried her. She thought of something to say that might interest them both: 'Miss Fox – I mean Eliot –' she paused to blush and then repeat the name, 'Eliot says air-conditioning gives her migraines.'

'That's impossible.' Her father did not turn to face her but addressed the passing traffic.

'Why?' asked Eliza.

'Yes, why?' Martha repeated, turning to query him.

Eliza did not wait for an answer but went on, 'Eliot says in New York it gets so hot there's a hot draught if you leave the window open.'

Clive opened his mouth. He seemed to be about to say, 'That's impossible', again.

'Eliot says—'

'Please stop repeating everything Eliot says,' he cut in. His voice was dry and cool as if it too had been conditioned.

Eliza was so surprised she could do nothing more than gape at him.

Martha put her fingertips to her eyebrow for a second, then took them away again and said, 'Clive—'

'What?' he rounded on her. 'Would it be too much to ask for a conversation about something other than Eliot fucking Fox?'

'Shut up, Dad!'

'Sit *down!*'

The driver braked and Eliza tipped in a heap to the carpeted floor of the cab. She yelped, 'Ow, my head!' and started to cry.

'Stop the cab!' Martha was frightened.

'I'm going to walk,' said Clive.

'No; we are.'

Martha scooped Eliza up off the floor and on to the pavement. She slammed the door behind them.

'She's *fine*,' said Clive out of the window. 'Stop making a fuss –' But his face was as white and frightened as Martha's.

The traffic lights changed and other cars began to hoot. The taxi sped away.

'I hate him I hate him,' Eliza said. 'My head hurts.'

'Ice-cream is good for hurting heads,' said Martha, and so they stopped at their change of buses for pancakes and ice-creams. They dawdled, eating at a café table and discussing Eliot.

'I wish she was here,' Eliza said. 'I wonder what flavour she would have. What kind of ice-cream did she eat in France?'

'It was a hundred years ago! I can't remember.'

'Oh, please, Mum, tell me more stuff.' Eliza was insatiable. 'Did she speak French as well as you? Did she wear nice clothes? Did she play the piano then?'

'Yes! Yes to all those things,' laughed Martha. 'Why don't you ask Tom about her? He was the one who really knew her.'

'He *loved* her,' gloated Eliza, licking the back of her spoon.

Back at the flat there was no sign of Clive. Martha said, 'I bet you he's gone for a run.'

Eliza checked the cupboard. 'Correct,' she said. 'No shoes. I hope he runs into a big *hole*. Hey, Mum –' she hung around Martha's neck for a moment, smackering the side of her mother's face with big, open kisses, 'I'm going downstairs to listen to my iPod' – *kiss* – 'Eliot gave me some clavier music to put on it' – *kiss-kiss* – 'That's another word for a piano.' She let go and scooted downstairs, calling over her shoulder, 'Tell Dad not to come and say goodnight. It's *bad*night.'

59

If it were just the two of us, Martha thought, smiling, *we could be like this always.*

This thought was an occasional, luxurious indulgence, like a chocolate truffle. She would only allow herself to daydream about a life without Clive if he gave her an excuse – if he had been nasty, as he had today. It did not happen often. Sometimes she wished it would, so that her fantasies might be excused, but Clive was a fair, decent and proper husband who did not often slip up. Today, however, he had been a bully. She wanted an apology.

First, however, she would treat herself to five minutes of an imaginary life. As she undressed for the shower – swallowed Nurofen – crouched to pee – she let a picture be illuminated in her head: herself and Eliza sharing a two-roomed flat, perhaps in Hampstead, perhaps near Eliot's house. Now she saw the three of them – Sunday breakfasts – walks on the Heath – back and forth to the school together. Naked, dreaming, she clambered under the water.

The pummel of it on the crown of her head brought her straight back to her senses. *No; no.* This was dizziness; silliness. She lathered bubbles up her legs and let water run over her face and into her eyes. *Wash wash wash.* She played the day back through her mind: taxi – Clive – angry – Eliot – mysterious – Eliza – adoring.

Drying herself, she felt a weariness; a confusion. She did not understand Eliza, not always. Why did she insist on listening to Mozart and making friends with her piano teacher? She knew why Eliza was bullied – anyone could see.

*

'They hate me,' Eliza had shrugged once, rubbing the tears from her eyes and the ribbons of snot from under her nose. 'They hate me when I'm good at something like maths, and they hate me when I'm rubbish – like at swimming. They just do.' It had been like this for so long that now she was matter-of-fact. 'In the wild there's always one animal left out. It usually dies.'

Hearing this had made Martha roar inside, like a lioness – *How dare they? My daughter!* – but it had also made her swallow as if something sharp had caught in her throat. During those many long nights that she had lain awake and worried about Eliza her conscience had accused her: *You. You were a tormenter.* She could remember the name – Suzy Milburn – of the girl in her class who had had to be taken away.

One night she had mewled in the dark and woken Clive to confess, but to her surprise he had not understood – or even tried to. 'Everyone's done something they regret,' he had said. 'You can't get upset about it for ever. It's not rational.'

'You haven't done anything bad,' Martha sobbed at him over the duvet. 'You don't know what it's like. I was mean – I was horrible – and I never said sorry.'

'You have to stop this,' said Clive, terse. 'It's pointless to punish yourself – for this or anything else.' He lay down again, facing the other way. 'Go back to sleep. I love you; Eliza loves you.' It was what tired people told each other in the middle of the night.

Dressing again, Martha thought about her husband. *Your breath smells.* He had been sneering. Bother Clive! She had not been drunk, she had been enjoying herself.

This was a moment to remind him that she was not a drunken layabout but a clever and valuable person. A contributor. Arranging herself at her desk she put on her headphones and immersed herself in the translation of a long document. An American voice recited into her ears, 'Section Four: Code of Conduct. This board requires at all levels impeccable values, honesty and openness. Through our processes we achieve transparent, open governance and communications under all circumstances with both performance and conformance addressed . . .' Martha's fingers flew over the keyboard and brought Arabic text to the screen.

When Clive walked into the flat he came and found her, still at her desk, and stood beside her chair. Martha took her headphones off and turned to face him. Clive looked at the screen for a moment as if for a prompt, but there was nothing written on it that he could understand. Then he looked at her. 'I'm sorry,' he said.

'You should be.'

'It's . . . work. It's an old case.'

'That's not good enough.'

But there was nothing more.

After a silence Clive said, 'Is Eliza OK? Shall I go in and say goodnight?'

'No. Leave her alone. She'll only get worked up again and you can see her in the morning.' After this, Martha picked up her headphones again. 'I've got to finish up here, so –'

Clive took the hint. 'OK,' he said, and went downstairs.

5

'Was everything all right, on Saturday?' Eliot asked Eliza when they were next seated together at the piano.

'Not really. Dad was weird. But then me and Mum got ice-creams on the way home.'

'What about now?'

'I don't know; I'm not speaking to him. Correction: I am speaking to him –' she counted on her fingers – 'I've said "fine" twice and "no" three times.'

This seemed to satisfy Eliot. She took a piece of paper from the top of the piano and gave it to Eliza. 'This is a concert that's happening on Friday evening,' she said. 'Would you like to go? With your parents? Or with me, if you like.'

'Mum and Dad hate classical music,' stated Eliza. 'They're always trying to make me turn it off.' She read aloud from the slip of paper: '*Carnival of the Animals* by Saint . . . who?'

'Saint Saëns,' pronounced Eliot.

'And, *The Young Person's Guide to the Orchestra* by Benjamin Britten.'

'There are instruments in the orchestra,' said Eliot, 'which are more sociable than the piano. It's not too late to start one – you could play with other people, you see, instead of always on your own.'

'I'm not always on my own,' Eliza said. 'Now there's you.' She looked up from the flyer. 'We could really go together?'

Eliza – being an intelligent and practical child – put the proposal to her mother in a manner which would produce the desired result: 'Eliot says is it OK if she takes me to a concert on Friday? Please please please, Mum. She's got two tickets and everything.'

'How exciting!' said Martha. 'I bet you'll have a lovely time.'

Now Eliza skipped around the room saying, 'Yay – yay – yay –'

If Eliza was delighted, then Martha must be pleased. She spread a smile on her face, but – *What is this?* – a feeling had surprised her: the sneaking tread of loneliness in her veins. *They don't want me.* She was startled by the press of this sensation and she tried to turn it away but on it came. *I will be left alone.* This was not right; this feeling was unjust; it was troubling and unwelcome and could not be allowed – she shook her head at herself – but now in its wake came something worse: a fearfulness which flooded her mind, staining it with an unexpected colour.

'They don't want me around,' Eliza had said of the girls in

her class. 'When I say something, it's wrong. I don't like the same stuff as them.'

'What sort of stuff?'

'Oh . . . *you* know. Everything.' Her voice had quavered. 'It doesn't matter,' she said after a moment. 'I don't mind doing things by myself.'

Martha had smoothed Eliza's ponytail with one hand. 'It won't always be like this,' she had said.

And now it was not.

Clive was not pleased about the concert and nor did he pretend to be. 'But I wanted to go to the cottage on Friday,' he said, thinking quickly and chewing his cereal in the kitchen. 'I thought we could have a weekend away.'

'Yes, let's,' said Martha. She was leaning on the counter, waiting for the kettle and eating muesli from the packet. The row of the weekend was not forgiven; she still did not like her husband enough to sit down at the table with him. 'You and I can go, Eliot can bring Eliza on Saturday, and we can ask Tom and the boys. We could surprise him with Eliot – I still haven't told him.' She rummaged in the packet for a nut. 'But – oh shit – what about the bats?'

Clive was reeling from the direction this conversation had taken. His mind had gone blank and he stared down at the bowl for inspiration. Playing for time, he cleared his throat. 'Bats?'

Lifting the kettle Martha said, 'For God's sake, Clive, what's the matter with you at the moment? The *bats*.'

Clive rummaged with his spoon. Where were the chips of banana? They were the only thing that had any flavour. 'We don't know anything about Eliot,' he said when he had composed himself. 'Are you happy for her to take Eliza? For the night? Home?'

Martha fired back: 'I wish she'd take me too.' She dunked her teabag and flipped it into the sink. Everything happened faster when she was irritated. 'Clive, we've known her since she was a kid and she's a teacher – do you know the sort of checks they have to run on those poor people? I'd never be allowed to work in a school.'

Clive was fighting the desire for a sudden, unspeakable violence. He wished he could pick up his cereal bowl and dash it against the wall – or against his own head – but instead he chose another weapon, and used it on his wife: 'No,' he said. 'You wouldn't. They're quite particular about mental health.' He chewed his mouthful with brisk attention.

Martha folded as if she had been struck. She struggled to reply. 'I can't believe you said that.' Then she slid away, down the stairs, and he heard the bedroom door click shut.

Clive crunched his breakfast. It made such a noise, in his mouth, and seemed to be taking for ever. At last he had swallowed it all, and then Eliza came pattering up the stairs for her Shreddies.

After her lunch – a bacon and avocado roll, a Snickers bar and a cup of tea – Belinda lay on the floor of her office for twenty minutes with a thick hardback book under her head.

'It's for my back,' she had told Clive the first time he discovered her. 'I broke it when I was a kid.'

'Falling out of a tree?' He had imagined a straw-haired, lawn-stained, country child.

'No. Jumping out of a window.' The statement had wiped his mind.

She lay quite still with her eyes shut and did not like to be disturbed, but today Clive had come to talk to her nonetheless, claiming special dispensation.

'I don't know what the hell I'm going to do,' he confessed. As he said it he felt better, but hearing it made him feel worse.

'"The only thing we have to fear",' Belinda quoted to him now, from the floor, '"is fear itself – nameless, unreasoning, unjustified terror which paralyses needed efforts to convert retreat into advance." Although in your case,' she continued in her normal voice, 'the fear is reasonable and justified.'

'Don't tell me what I already know,' Clive pleaded. 'Tell me what to do.'

'I've told you: wait for Eliot to tell and deny it, or tell Martha yourself.'

'Eliot said she wouldn't tell. "I won't have to" – that's what she said.'

'Don't you see? She doesn't have to tell. You're going to fall apart.'

Clive was silent. Was Belinda enjoying this? Seeing him cornered? He was afraid and he wanted help but there was no refuge here. Belinda seemed to be unfurling a banner that did not protest his innocence but instead proclaimed his crimes.

Now she pressed her fingertips together over her chest as if she were a medieval lady on a church tomb. 'You're in a hole,

Clive. No two ways about it.' She spoke with relish; he could not doubt it any longer. This was unpleasant, Clive thought, and upsetting. He would not mention it again.

Miss Fox – Eliot, now that they were friends – had made school better. Just at the moment, in fact, school was nicer than home: her parents were still having an argument – a silent one – and Eliza did not like to be in the same room as them both.

Her father came to sit on her bed and talk about the concert. 'Wouldn't you rather come to the cottage with us?' he said. 'I haven't seen you all week.'

Eliza said nothing. *Because you've been working every night until bedtime*, she was thinking.

Every evening she had expected her father to come to her room, but he had not. She had heard him treading the floor-boards in the kitchen above her head until she had either put on her headphones or fallen asleep. Now he was here, not to tell her he was sorry but to forbid her from doing what she most wanted. She knew that when he said, 'Wouldn't you rather?', it meant, 'I want you to change your mind'.

She frowned at the duvet. He was being unfair, she knew he was, but nonetheless he had brought guilt into the room with him and it was snouting and curling a place for itself on the bed. She pushed it away, cross and determined: if her father were going to shove, she would have to shove him back.

'We will come, on Saturday. Like Mum said we could. Please, Dad,' she appealed. 'Eliot's my friend.'

'She's not your friend, she's your teacher.' This came in a different voice. 'We *pay* her to teach you the piano. A friend would be a little girl your own age who liked spending time with you.'

'Eliot does.' Eliza was on the edge of tears – this was worse than the playground.

'Eliza love,' Martha came in, 'have you done your teeth?' She looked at them both, and stayed at the door. 'What's going on?'

'Dad's being horrible.'

Later Eliza heard Martha shout, 'What is your fucking problem?' all in one breath.

The front door slammed. Eliza wondered who had gone out and her heart fluttered in her chest. She hoped it was her father and when she heard his shoes clop down the front steps to the road she was relieved.

Mum came into the room and said, 'I said you can go and you can. I'll deal with Dad. But don't mention it to him again, OK?'

Eliza swallowed. In a mouse's voice she said, 'OK.'

The end of the week arrived. Clive sat in his office and brooded. He fingered crisps from a packet on the desk and into his mouth where he let each one rest on his tongue like a communion wafer. When the caustic sting of flavouring began to burn, he crunched and swallowed.

He liked this sensation – it was absorbing and short-lived. He liked to think of such things as crisps, a headache, or the weather. He liked to wonder if it would rain, and whether he would be caught out when it did. He liked the thoughts which bobbed at the surface, but not the shapes that lurked on the ocean floor.

*

Carcasses on the seabed rotted in the end – he and Eliza had once watched a programme about a dead whale. 'Gross . . .' Eliza had said, her eyes like saucers and her face lit blue by the screen. 'And amazing.'

Clive tried to remember the peace of a life before Eliot. Eliza had, that morning, avoided talking to him again. 'How long are you going to keep this up?' he had asked her. She had continued to eat her Shreddies, wearing her earphones and staring straight ahead. The silence was as clear a sound as if she had told him to get stuffed.

Clive had said to Martha, 'Eliza wears those things all the time.'

'Yes,' Martha had replied.

'She can't hear a word I say.'

'No.'

She had said nothing else, and Clive had left to catch the Tube.

With a blink Clive turned his thoughts instead to the weather.

'Got your brolly?' the man in the corner shop had asked, cheerfully handing Clive his change. 'It's going to piss down all afternoon, apparently.'

Rain was a nuisance. Martha and Eliza – driving straight from the school gates – would be halfway to the cottage by now, but Clive had to cross London to get to the station and he risked a soaking. He did not fancy sitting on the train in a puddle, and other people smelled of charity shops when they were wet.

Outside the window the square dimmed from a gloomy afternoon to a night dark, a cupboard-dark, as if the sun had not set but had been shut out by a closed door. Painted railings seemed to shine and window frames to glow, as they did at dusk. One front door turned the blood-soaked red of a toadstool and another the pungent milk-green of a mouldering corpse. There would – there must – be a storm. A dreadful silence had fallen and the whole lidded city seethed with static.

Clive shifted from his seat to throw his rubbish away and to stand and stare at the window, wiping his hands on a napkin. He felt the creep and prickle of sweat under his hair.

The sky split with a flash and a simultaneous *crack-gulp-boom* of thunder that made the building – and everyone in it – jump with nerves. 'Christ almighty,' Clive heard Belinda say in the corridor. From others came fearful laughs and exclamations.

The trees in the square – broad, sobbing planes – lifted the ends of their fingers all at once as a squall of wind caught their leaves underneath. A noise came from them, a great and glorious shushing like a wave pouring in over shingle.

There followed a series of flat thunderclaps and then, after a short silence, a murderous-sounding crackle. Clive was afraid – not of the storm but of something at large in the air, something coming to catch him in its claws. His shirt clung to his ribs. He would go – he would go now. He slammed out of the door, hurried to the Underground, plunged down the steps and scampered into the fug.

He was just in time. On the other side of London he emerged to find the city under a downpour and the station a slippery rink of puddles and newspaper pages. His train-carriage windows were sluiced by rain and steamed with vapour.

It took a small disaster for commuters to make friends: people clucked, laughed and shook out their clothes.

'Soaked!'

'Drenched!'

'Right down to my knickers!'

Clive, dry as a bone, stared and listened from his seat. *Why did I not get wet?* He did not feel blessed but cursed: condemned to a ghost-like solitude.

Part III

6

Clive had not intended to go to Eliot's birthday party but
when the day came he found himself at his parents'
home – on a laundry run – and with nothing to do that night.
Tom was there, excited and jumpy about the evening to come,
and Clive was jealous.

Tom had not given up on Eliot and still loved her, not quite
hopeless and not quite encouraged. 'That naughty Eliot,'
sighed Val. 'She leads him on, poor Tom.'

Clive had not told his brother about the day at the races. It
would have been uncomfortable to tell and hard for Tom to
hear, so he kept it to himself – quite tight against his chest.

Watching Tom bob about in the kitchen, bothering his
mother and making her laugh, Clive could read his brother's
mind – they all could: *Perhaps tonight.*

'I might come too,' Clive offered. When he saw Tom's
surprised face turn towards him he knew that he did want to

go. 'Yes, I think I'll come with you, to the party. She asked me, did you know that?'

Tom pulled no punches: it was his big night and he did not want his brother there. 'She asked you because she thinks you're a sad act with no friends. She's not expecting you to actually come. Anyway, what about exams? What about revising?'

'I'll take the night off.'

Tom sat down at the kitchen table to lace his sneaker and did not say anything for a moment. Val looked from one son to the other but kept quiet. When Tom straightened up he said, 'But –' He stopped and started again. 'But everyone will be my age – apart from her parents. You won't know anyone. It'll be weird.'

Clive stared at his reflection in the kitchen mirror. 'Eliot said there were all sorts of different people going,' he said.

Other grown-ups, was what she had laughed down the telephone. *There might even be some as old as you. Hey – and listen: have you got a number for Danny?* The words had struck and winded him.

'You'll probably chat up her mum or something,' continued Tom. 'You're all right when you're with Martha, but on your own you can be a bit ... ' The sentence did not seem to have an end.

Martha had gone to visit her father. 'He sounded awful on the phone,' she had confessed to Clive that morning. 'He sounded wasted.' She had filled Viv's car with provisions – 'I bet he hasn't eaten proper food in weeks' – and pressed away through the Saturday traffic.

She would have been baffled by Clive's change of plan. 'Eliot's birthday party? But why?'

I don't have to tell her everything, Clive reasoned with his conscience.

The two brothers shouted "Bye Mum,' over their shoulders as they went out of the front door and Clive heard, 'Send her our love—' before the door slammed.

They cycled to the station, tied up their bikes and caught the Tube.

'It's nice up here,' said Tom as they walked towards Primrose Hill. 'I'm going to live in Camden when I'm older.'

Tom was in love with everything about Eliot, thought Clive, and that included her family home and her postcode.

Martha had been right when she had said that Kilburn and Primrose Hill were separated by more than geography. Eliot's was a sturdy, square white cake of a house that stood, quite certain of itself and its position, in a proper garden of its own. From a glossy front door, stone steps led to a gate at the pavement.

Inside, Clive was given champagne and Tom a glass of punch. 'Punch for the young,' trilled Sabrina, Eliot's mother. 'Darling Tom,' she added, kissing him. 'How's my rotten daughter treating you? I wish you were in love with *me*.' She sighed and shimmered away in her silk drapery.

'Nightmare woman,' said Tom, shaking his head. 'She showed me her bush, once. It was unbelievably massive.' Then he sidled off to have his drink topped up by a friend.

When Eliot saw Clive she said, 'Clive!' as if he were the only person she had wanted to come to the party. She was glassy-eyed and dazed; starstruck with herself.

A couple of hard-faced girlfriends had taken charge of her, holding her by the elbows and steering her round the house. The two friends stared and giggled at Clive, flirted with Eliot's father and gazed with unblinking insolence at Sabrina before spotting Tom and separating him from the crowd, like mute, efficient sheepdogs. They herded him up the stairs in front of them and away to Eliot's room.

Tom did not try to win people over but with an unconscious, careless, laughing kindness he attracted them. His mother had called it his 'magnet'.

'It's because he's free,' Martha had said, watching Tom on the beach. 'You can tell a mile off.'

Now, as Tom was carried off upstairs by the sheepdogs, Clive felt conflicting thoughts strike him within like bits of flint: *Those girls look mean – I wish they liked me – But they like Tom – I don't care anyway.* In the days before Martha that sensation – rummaging; cutting – had come often.

As Tom had suspected, Clive did not know anyone here. He became aware that he was caught in a hopeless position: he did not wish to be dismissed by the teenagers as a boring grown-up but nor did he wish to be seen by the adults as an ignorant schoolboy. He wanted his own category: *Oxford finalist.*

He discovered that if he walked into a room where adults stood in discussion he was regarded with cool disinterest. In the basement, teenagers looked up at him with incurious distrust

78

from their draped positions over beanbags and cushions on the floor.

He located Eliot's bedroom: a shut door, a stink of fags, a noisy hubbub within. Clive knocked and pushed the door open a crack.

'Who is it?' said an unfamiliar voice. Clive could see through the chink three girls lying pressed together like sardines across the bed. One of them held a bottle of vodka.

'Clive. Can I come in?'

A whispered consultation and then, 'No!', shouted in unison. The door was kicked shut in his face and he heard their shrieks of laughter.

Clive was feverish with discomfort and a needling terror. If Martha had been there she would have told him to go home. 'Why stay?' she would have said. 'You're hating it; you're miserable.' *Give up*, he told himself. *Go home. No one will care – no one will even notice.* Never mind his dignity; he wanted his bed.

The decision made, Clive felt a great relief. He opened the front door and took a breath of the clean, bright night—

'Clive?'

He peered into the garden. 'Danny?'

A tall figure, lit cigarette glowing between his teeth, was stepping up to the door with a click of his soles. 'Leaving already?'

'No,' lied Clive. 'Just going to get some fags for Eliot.'

'I've got loads,' came the reply, and somehow Clive was inside the house again with the door shut behind him and a brand new drink in his hand.

Danny moved with presidential confidence from room to room and Clive trod in his shadow like the lowly ambassador. Sabrina was greeted with a warm kiss on each cheek and the gentle clasp of a hand at her elbow. 'Stunning,' murmured Danny to her and then, 'How are you? Are they behaving themselves? Has anyone broken the law?'

'Probably.' Sabrina giggled. 'Have you seen Eliot? She'll be so glad you're here.'

'I came back to see you,' said Danny, gazing down at her. 'Eliot can wait.' His voice was glycerine-coated and his hand drifted to her waist.

If she had had a tail, Sabrina would have whisked it. Clive, listening to their exchange and staring into the fireplace, thought he might be sick. He pictured a torrent of vomit quenching the blue gas flames. He allowed himself a fantasy: a jet of flame; her dress alight; Danny torched and squealing and he, Clive, laughing and laughing, all the way home on the Tube. He took a speculative suck at his drink.

When Sabrina had departed, tipsy with compliments, to check on the caterers, Clive asked Danny, 'How come you two are such pals?'

Danny took a gold lighter off the mantelpiece and examined it. 'I met her earlier. I dropped a present round for Eliot, and Sabrina gave me some cake. Where's Martha?'

Clive did not answer but asked, 'What present?'

Eliot interrupted them, coiling around Danny like a vapour. 'Danny Danny Danny! You came back!'

'I said I would,' he said. 'Happy sixteenth birthday – again.'

Eliot took his hand. 'Sweet sixteen,' she said, blinking up at him, 'but not for long.'

Danny laughed. 'Oh yes? Which of these poor sods have you set your sights on?'

But Eliot just twisted his fingers in hers and gazed at him. Then she said, 'Come on,' and took his drink from his hand. She passed the glass to Clive and led Danny away, downstairs towards the dance floor.

Clive bobbed in the swirled air left behind them, trying to stay afloat. Eliot wanted Danny – it was plain – but wanted what? Putting the drinks down on a side table he turned to see Tom, standing at the bottom of the stairs.

'Where did Eliot go?' Tom asked Clive with a helpless look.

'Downstairs.' They both went down to watch Eliot dance round Danny. She held her hands above her head and twisted round him, glittering and luminous. Danny did not respond but only danced. He made no move to touch her and Eliot, trying to tease, floated towards him and away again.

If Danny could not – would not – see what Eliot wanted, Tom could. After a few minutes he lifted his shoulders from the wall he had been leaning on and, defeated, leaned towards his brother. 'I'm going to go,' he shouted into Clive's ear.

Clive followed him up the stairs. 'You can't,' he bleated. 'What about me?'

'I'm not going home,' said Tom. 'I just took half an E. I'll go round the corner to a mate's. He's gone already, taken some people.'

'Is Eliot on drugs?' Clive asked. 'Should I be worried?'

'No, just pissed. She doesn't do drugs.' He picked up his

jacket from the couch in the hall. 'See you at home,' he said, 'tomorrow.' And then he was gone.

Clive stood in the hall and wondered what to do. The grown-ups had left, the caterers' van had disappeared from the driveway and Eliot's parents had retired to what Sabrina referred to as 'The Orangery' – an annexe in their garden which was 'about ten times nicer than our actual house,' according to Tom. There seemed to be no one to take things in hand. Was he the only one who could see what might happen? If Eliot got into real trouble, who would care?

Fretting, Clive trailed back downstairs but both Eliot and Danny had vanished. The music played to a near-empty room and he stood and stared at the place where they had danced. In this slow moment he pictured them locked together on a sofa, perhaps in the drawing room, surrounded by framed photographs of Eliot as a younger child. With a burst of frenzied energy – breath coming in gasps – he flung himself around the house, opening and shutting doors.

In a small study he found Danny sitting in an armchair while two girls – the sheepdogs – lay on the rug, sharing a spliff and giggling at MTV.

'Hello, Clive,' said Danny. 'Look at these two – they're wasted.'

'Where's Eliot?'

'I don't know.' Danny looked at him, puzzled. 'Are you all right?'

Clive could not contain himself. 'It depends,' he spat at Danny, 'on what's happened.'

'What do you mean?'

'Oh come on, Danny – you know what I mean. I saw the way you were dancing with Eliot.'

There was a brief pause while Danny looked Clive full in the face, his expression of astonishment curdling to contempt. Clive held his ground but he could feel a hot flush creep up his throat. The girls, oblivious, continued to giggle, yawn and grapple like tired puppies.

'You're pathetic,' said Danny. 'You're a joke.' He turned back to the girls and the television screen.

Clive tried again. 'If you so much as –'

Danny did not respond – he did not react at all – and Clive withdrew, closing the door behind him.

Treading slowly upstairs through the house he watched each foot lift from one step to the next. He had got it all wrong. He should never have come. *On your own you can be a bit . . .* Tom was right.

'You've got to go home,' he said to his reflection in the window on the landing, but another voice spoke in his head: *I'll say goodbye to Eliot, and then I'll go.* He turned to climb the next flight of stairs.

In answer to his knock at the bedroom door came a muffled sound that might have been, 'Who is it?' Clive, with a responsible adult's sense of concern, pushed open the door of the room and stepped inside. He found Eliot collapsed on the bed with clothes and hair twisted in a bundle around her like a bird's nest that had tumbled from a hedge into the road.

The room was silent and still – the close-knit air of a London attic. Clive closed the door behind him and exhaled. The pounding in his ears subsided.

'Eliot?' he said. 'It's me, Clive. Are you all right?'

'Clive –' A hand stuck out towards him from the middle of the nest. There was a stifled sob and then Eliot said, 'I've been such an idiot.'

'What's happened?'

'I wanted . . . it was so embarrassing. I love him so much. I can't believe . . . and now we'll never be friends. He wouldn't . . . he didn't want to . . . ' She faltered on the words.

So: Danny had turned her down. Clive waited for the softening sensation of relief but to his surprise he felt again that strike of flint within.

She was devastated. He wanted to console her – he told himself to – but he struggled to muster sympathy, even to his voice. 'I'm sorry,' he managed to say. 'Poor you.'

'I told everyone.' Eliot was crying now, in a series of sniffs and hiccups. 'Everyone knew I wanted him to be the one . . . everyone's going to think I'm such an idiot . . . '

'No one thinks you're an idiot,' Clive said. 'Tom was just a bit sad, that's all.'

'Poor Tom,' she said with a gulp. 'Oh, God, poor Tom . . . I'm such a bitch to him. Is he still here?' She lifted her head with a hopeful look at the door.

'No,' said Clive firmly. 'He's gone to another party.'

'I've blown it,' said Eliot. 'My birthday party. What a joke.'

'It was great,' said Clive, but it sounded lame and insubstantial. After a pause he added, 'And I think you're great.'

There was no response to this and then in a small voice she said, 'Do you?'

'Yes,' said Clive. He trusted the tone of his voice: avuncular; certain. *The poor little thing*, he thought, *being rejected like that.* He raised his eyes from the heap on the bed and looked around the room.

His eye was caught by the coat that Danny had given Eliot that day at the races – the only piece of clothing not in a tangle on the floor. It had been straightened on to a hanger and hung from the curtain pole. The sight of it struck Clive with as much force as if Danny himself had been standing in the room looking down at them with his tall certainty, his glamour and his fatal magnetism. *He's a total bastard*, Martha and Viv had said.

Clive felt weary, defeated and alone. 'Goodnight, Eliot,' he said. 'I'm going to head off home.'

But again the hand reached from its knitted blur of twigs and stretched towards him. 'Don't go,' she said. 'It's my birthday – well,' she corrected herself, 'it was.' She shifted her cheek on the pillow. 'So drunk ... stupid ... tired ...' Her voice could only be a moment from sleep.

She tugged at Clive's hand and he sat down on the edge of her bed and looked at the formless tumble of her, lying there. 'Shall I take your shoes off?' he asked. 'Your feet'll be murder tomorrow if you sleep in them.'

'Oh, go on then.' It was a mumble. 'May as well ... Not going back downstairs.'

She was lying on her side and Clive reached round and pulled off her shoes, one after the other. He dropped them on to the floor. 'You're wearing a dress,' he said in a slow voice, looking down at her. 'I don't think I've ever seen you in a dress.'

'Whaddya think?' she slurred.

'Very pretty,' said Clive. With an absent-minded gesture he pulled its hem down over her calves.

After a little pause Eliot muttered into the pillow, 'Don't say "pretty"; say "sexy".'

There was a silence which to Clive was filled with noise. He looked down at her ankles, crossed on the bed, and the red marks her shoes had left on her feet. He moved his hand from the hem of her dress to her uppermost foot and with his thumb he rubbed at the bruised skin.

'... Feels nice ...' came Eliot's voice, but it was just a murmur.

She did not stir again for a moment or two and Clive stared down at his thumb, moving to and fro across her skin, just an inch one way and then back, and away, and back. It seemed to be the only thing moving in the world.

'Mm,' repeated Eliot. 'That feels nice.'

When he heard those words again, Clive instructed himself to stop this little movement.

Eliot still had the fingers of Clive's other hand clasped between hers. She did not let go but turned her wrist until their two palms were pressed together. Their fingers slid between each other's and linked securely into place. At the same time, with the smallest motion, she shifted her foot until it was not just resting under his hand but docked in his palm. *How did that happen?* Clive wondered, looking down. *I have not moved.*

He seemed now to be holding her at two points, by hand and foot, and now she turned towards him, stirring and unfolding like a sheaf of papers at the breath of a breeze.

Back in the hall he found Danny, trying on one of Sabrina's straw sunhats and admiring his image in the hall mirror.

Seeing Clive's reflection in the glass behind him, Danny said, 'Is Eliot all right?'

'Eliot?' repeated Clive.

'She was so pissed. I thought she might have made herself ill, or got in trouble—'

'Trouble?'

'—with her parents.' Danny adjusted the brim of the hat.

'I don't know,' said Clive. 'I went up to have a slash.' When the throb of the lie had died away in the air he said, 'I'm going to go home.'

'Are you? Me too.' With the hat still on his head Danny followed Clive out of the front door.

They stood on the pavement for a moment. Danny yawned a tiger's yawn and stretched. Clive stared at him, unseeing. All his faculties seemed to have been disabled; he felt like an automaton; he was not sure he could even have given a name to himself or to the day.

It was going to be a grubby sort of dawn. It felt cold to him now but the day would be hot. It felt clammy but he knew it would not rain. It was dark but soon the city would be pressed beneath the palm of a white, accusing sky.

He said, 'I think I'll walk to Finchley Road,' and glanced at his watch. 'It'll be the first train in a minute.'

'All right, mate,' said Danny. He stuck out his hand. 'See you around.'

'Where are you going to go?' said Clive, curious.

'I'll walk over to my girlfriend's,' said Danny. 'She's in Camden.'

Girlfriend? Clive wanted to shout at him and punch him in the face. *Girlfriend?* 'You should have brought her,' he said in a level voice.

'She's got kids,' said Danny, 'and no one to babysit.' He raised the hat in farewell. 'G'night.'

Clive crept to the station, fox-like, along the darkest gutters and gunnels of the pavement.

Stowed in his seat on the empty train he stared at his reflection in the opposite window, billowing and diminishing in the glass. At one moment his face was a monstrous distortion – the face of a cheat – and at another it had shrunk to a freakish pebble – the face of a coward. Guilt rattled at the carriage doors – leaped and snapped at the flying wheels – chattered in his ears – pounded at his head. The train swept through the tunnels.

What have I done? What have I done?

'Oh, no –' Blinking, fearful, Eliot had spoken afterwards as if she had only just woken and found him there. 'Oh no – Tom; Martha –' She had shrunk away from him, furling the bedclothes around herself. 'You've got to go ... Go, please; *now*. If my dad or my mum ... you've *got to go*, Clive –' Her voice had risen, tightened and trembled at the point of tears.

She had not needed to say it. Clive had known that this was no place for him to stay. He did not belong in that single bed, amid that heap of discarded clothes. In that little room a poster curled on the wall, luminous stars glowed on the ceiling and the coat glared down from on high like a hovering angel.

As Clive pulled on his shoes a heavy pulse beat in his veins and against his temples. He listened and was afraid, as if that sound was the footfall on the stairs.

On the train, when he closed his eyes, it was Martha's face he saw. If he tried to banish it there was his brother's, in its place. Tom's expression – desolate – as he had shrugged his way out of the door. 'She likes that other bloke,' he had said sadly to Clive. 'Your friend.'

Martha – Tom – Martha – Tom

Eliot – Eliot – Eliot.

Emerging from the dark – pummelling through the suburbs – Clive was relieved to find his ballooning image erased by the dark rushing blur of cutting walls – violet brick; blue-green ivy – under a lightening dawn sky.

But try as he might to see it differently the world looked as damp and soiled as a pile of old laundry, waiting for its turn in the wash. It might be doomsday out there. The sun might never come up.

Tom could not be certain why Eliot did not want to be friends with him anymore, but he guessed at the reason: 'It was that man – your friend. Something must have happened, after I left.' His words clawed at Clive's insides.

Eliot stopped answering the telephone. Although her mother took Tom's messages and promised to pass them on, Eliot did not ring him back. Tom puzzled, suffered and agonised in turn. It was his first abandonment; he did not take it well. 'I never should have gone home,' he said to Clive. 'I'll kill that man if I ever see him again.'

'Poor Tom,' was Martha's comment, 'but it was bound to happen. Eliot's trouble – I could have told him that.'

Clive knew about trouble. He knew what had happened. He knew how Eliot was.

Her letter arrived at College on the morning of his first exam; he collected it from his pigeonhole. He saw the handwritten envelope and thought it was a good luck card.

When he had read the note he tore the paper into pieces, lengthways and crossways, and then scrunched the pieces into a ball with his fist. He dropped the bundle into a litter bin on the pavement. He stood and stared at the bin until a bus came past him too close and the blast of air made him stumble.

After having gaped and mimed his way through the exam, he wrote a letter in reply.

'You're back late,' said Martha in the evening when he returned. 'How was it?'

'What?'

'How was the exam?' She looked at him again. 'Are you all right?'

'Yes, fine. A bit tired. It was ... not too bad, I think.' Clive had no recollection of what the questions had been, or how he had answered them. He marvelled at this new person, this new Clive, who could cheat and lie with such fluency.

A second letter arrived just as exams were over. This time Clive recognised the slant of Eliot's writing and her blue felt tip; a sharp tug seemed to loose his heart from its casing. He was on his way to celebrate with Martha but when he saw the waiting envelope he collected it and made a diversion to the public toilets by the town hall. He locked himself into a cubicle and stood with his back to the door.

The smell of disinfectant skinned his lungs and brought him to a new, acute wakefulness, as if he had been rubbed raw. Holding the note between fastidious fingertips – his pummelling heart colliding against his ribs – he read the contents:

Clive -
Thank you very much for the money. The abortion didn't
cost that much so I'm going to spend the rest on getting
wasted. This is also to let you know that you are scum, I
hate your guts and I hope you rot in hell.
- Eliot

Clive waited to see what would happen – perhaps he would weep or beat the wall of the cubicle with his fists – but the curious thing was that nothing happened at all. He stirred inside himself with a poker. Nothing but cold ashes. He felt exactly as he had before.

After a few moments he tore the letter into small pieces and threw them into the toilet bowl in front of him. Then he pulled the chain and stood and watched until they had all been flushed away.

7

Everyone agreed that the stairs were dangerous, but Val pronounced them 'lethal' and condemned the whole flat as 'hopeless for children'. One Sunday afternoon Clive fitted a child's safety gate at each end so that a tottering Eliza would not plummet from the kitchen to the basement. The next time his mother asked him whether he had 'done something about those dreadful stairs', he was able to crow, 'Yes, Mum, so you never need ask me again.'

'You've no idea what toddlers are like,' Val said. 'They move like lightning.'

'What do you want us to do, chop off her legs?'

'Don't be silly. It's *those* stairs – they're too steep. The way they just fall out of the kitchen floor like that . . . It's not right; it's all upside-down. I'd feel better if the kitchen were downstairs and the bedrooms upstairs, like in a normal house.'

'It's normal for a flat,' defended Clive. 'Stop fussing.'

*

Eliza did not move like lightning, Clive thought, she moved like a crab on roller-skates. Skeetering over the floor with amazing rapidity her gait was both crawling and walking; forwards and sideways. Bottom in the air, palms on the ground, one eye cocked towards him and one to the floorboards as if she were waiting for the starter's pistol. To watch her made him smile – but he had to be careful: if he took too much obvious pleasure in their daughter, it would set Martha's temper alight. 'You wouldn't find her so bloody sweet if you'd sat on the bus for an hour with her screaming in your ear.'

Clive needed to take particular care this evening because he had some news for Martha which – although nothing to do with Eliza – he knew would spark her fury. Back early from work he waited for them in the kitchen, watching the street from the window, and prepared his announcement in his head.

'You're a lucky motherfucker,' Justin had said to him in the office that day. 'You've scored the Manhattan trip: two nights in a hotel and everything on expenses.' Justin had been jealous. 'It fucks me off,' he had said. 'A trip like this is wasted on you: you're *married* with a *baby*.'

'So that's it for me, is it? No more fun of any kind?'

'There's no point – you can't enjoy yourself. All parents ever want to do, when they get away from their kids, is sleep.'

But after making further enquiries Justin had discovered a drawback which had set his mind at rest. 'Bad luck, mate,' he had crowed. 'You're going with Battleaxe Galacticunt.' This was his name for Belinda Easton, one of their seniors, in whom he had a peculiar ghoulish interest. 'I bet she keeps her tights on when she's having sex,' he had once remarked.

It was not so much this comment – or the others like it – which made Clive want to hold Justin's face over a flame, but the yawning, dreary expectation of them: that Justin should slip so snugly into the role of office misogynist and that Belinda Easton, powerful and plain, should be his target.

Clive would have surrendered the trip if he could – he knew he would not enjoy it. He had never liked to go away, and least of all now. Seeing Martha yank the buggy up the front steps from the pavement, he turned with apprehension to the door.

The front door banged shut. He heard the sound of the buggy jousting with the bicycles in the corridor. Martha's key turned in the lock and now the flat door flew open, striking the wall behind it with a smart, vigorous punch. Martha, taking no notice, pushed past its returning swing with the buggy's front wheels as if she were driving an icebreaker. She pummelled through the hall – 'These fucking coats!' – and let the door slam behind her. The buggy was hung with straining shopping bags and inside it sat Eliza, squalling and squirming in her straps.

Clive hesitated for two beats – *one, two* – and then stepped forward to greet them. As he kissed Martha on her marbled cheek she said, 'D'you know what's been the most useful thing about a First in Arabic from Oxford? Respect on the Uxbridge Road.' She might have been joking – she would have been once, when she had worked and he had been learning the law – but today, to be on the safe side, he said nothing.

95

He crouched to unbuckle Eliza who, stripped of her water-proofs and plonked on the floor, started scooting from one side of the room to the other, chuntering and muttering with relief and contentment. Clive glanced at the shut gate – *There's no point having it and leaving it open* – and Martha paced tight circles round the kitchen.

With cautious interest Clive inquired, 'How was the film?'

Martha and Eliza had been to a 'Cinemama' screening at the multiplex. 'What film?' said Martha. 'All I heard was screaming.'

'What about the other –' he had been going to say 'mothers', but instead he said '– parents?'

'Zombies and morons,' she said. 'As usual.'

'They can't *all* be.' Clive tried to be reasonable. 'Not every mother you ever meet.'

Martha gave a mirthless laugh. 'Why don't you go next time, if you don't believe me? They're all about forty, for one thing, and they're so bloody grateful to have a baby it's *pathetic*.'

In the old days, Clive might have laughed at this.

'I'm so bored I think I'm losing my mind,' said Martha, her voice as bleak as winter. 'It's killing me.'

'Come on, you're being—'

'What? I'm being *what*?' she challenged him, but he did not go on. 'If I have to carry on doing this much longer I'll ...' She left the threat open: a window through which she might fly.

'We always said after Christmas,' Clive tried to appease her. 'It's not long.'

Martha was silent.

Clive went on, 'It can't make that much difference, can it? We're all set up for January. You can't get a job between now and Christmas. What would you do?'

'I'd rather fold T-shirts in GAP than do this.'

Clive seemed to chew and swallow several other words before saying only, 'You don't mean that.'

'Don't tell me what I do and don't mean,' snarled Martha at him. 'If it paid more than getting a nanny, I'd do it. I'd clean the bogs at Terminal One on Christmas Eve if I thought it would get me out of this hell.'

A silence, then, 'Please don't say things like that,' Clive begged her.

Martha walked out of the room.

She used to cry and say, 'I'm a bad mother. I hate it. Why do I hate it?'

Clive had no answer to this question but he would try to placate her. 'Neither of us knows how to do this. Everyone finds parenting difficult. Even Mum says the first year is hard.'

Once she shouted at him, all on one note like the blast of an oncoming truck, 'Don't mention your fucking mother again!'

And once she said in a whisper, 'You don't find it hard.' It was an accusation, and it was true. Clive was wonderful with Eliza; everyone said so.

This evening he gave Eliza her bath, kneeling beside the tub and sprinkling water from a toy watering can over her head and her tummy to make her laugh.

Martha spoke from the doorway. 'I don't understand her,' she said. 'I don't understand what she's saying, but you do.' She had been watching them.

Her voice startled Clive, who had thought she was upstairs, but he turned around and gave her a careful smile. She did not return it, saying only, 'I thought I was supposed to be the one with language skills.'

'Come and join in?' pleaded Clive, wet arms dangling in the tub and shirt sleeves rolled over his elbows.

'No,' said Martha. Then again, more quietly, 'No.' She shouldered herself off the wall and turned away.

After putting Eliza to bed Clive showered and then, weary, climbed the stairs to the kitchen. When she heard his footsteps Martha said, 'You'll be wanting your dinner now, I expect?'

In the days when she had worked and he had been taking exams this had been a joke: 'Where's my tea?' He had worked at the kitchen table every day – books spread out all round him and his head full of the law – and in the evenings he had been roused by the front door's slam, Martha's feet in the hall and her key in the lock. Into the room she would blow like a summer wind, dropping her bag on the floor and her hands on his shoulders, leaning down to kiss him. Her cold, fresh, outdoor face would be pressed against his – he could feel it now, the push of her grin – and she would growl, 'Where's my tea?'

Now she was chopping an onion with a controlled but visible fury that quaked the air around her.

'We could get a takeaway, if you like?' he said it in a cautious voice.

'It's a bit late for that,' she said. 'I've been chopping onions for a fucking hour.' She clashed the saucepan on to the hob and sparked the gas, over and over. 'Come on, you little bastard,' she murmured at the cooker.

Clive breathed, in and out. 'Let's have a glass of wine.'

When they had eaten in front of the television, Martha lifted the sash of the window and sat beside it to smoke a cigarette. Clive looked at her profile, staring out into the dark. Only one half of her face – that face he loved so much – was visible to him. Hesitant, nervous, he began, 'I've got to go to New York.'

She turned her head, unblinking, like an owl on a branch. 'What?'

'Just for a day or so. It's an American client. We've got to go through some documents ... I'm just going as an assistant, really, to help the woman in charge of the case.'

Martha turned back to the window and inhaled a drag on her cigarette. 'When?'

'The day after tomorrow. For two nights.'

'Lucky you,' she said. 'Hotel, business-class flights, room service, pretty ladies bringing you things on trays ... It'll be a real holiday.'

Clive said nothing. It was better not to; her calm tone did not deceive him. 'When I get back,' he said, 'let's go away for the weekend. We'll leave Eliza with Mum and Dad.'

'And give your mum another opportunity to tell me what a shit parent I am? No thanks.'

'She's never said that.' Clive kept his tone neutral. 'All she said was that since you hadn't known your own mother it was bound to be more difficult—'

'I know what she said.'

That voice! Gravel thrown at a window.

Clive shut his eyes and continued, dogged, on his path. 'Anyway, let's go away. Shall we? For a break. And some sleep. We could go to Wales, do some walking.'

'Wales?' she laughed. 'Yes, when I'm sitting here with the baby I dream of going to Wales and walking up mountains.'

Clive took a deep breath. 'Well, what would you like to do instead?'

He knew she would not reply. This was where the conversation always ended. They both knew what Martha wanted but the words were too terrible to be said and instead hung in the air like the smell of her tobacco smoke: *I want to run away; I want to leave you both; I want to have my life again.*

She had run away once, but had come back crying in the morning to find Clive and Eliza breakfasting together as if she had never existed. Both had looked round, when they heard the door, with the same expression: cold and disappointed. It was the way her father had looked when she had come home from school with any grade less than an 'A'.

'I knew you'd be back,' Clive had said. He had not meant to reassure but to punish. 'Take over, will you?' He had put down Eliza's plastic spoon, got to his feet and left, shutting the door behind him with a careful click that said, *I can keep my temper.*

The room had settled to quiet after his departure, mother and daughter staring at each other in silence. *She doesn't know me*, Martha thought, panicking. Then had come what she dreaded most, much more than not being recognised: Eliza had widened her eyes, trembled, glanced at the door and begun to cry in loud, dragging caws like a hungry rook abandoned in its nest.

These were the punishing moments that Clive did not see – moments that stretched into hours and days – when just to be alone with her mother seemed enough to make Eliza desperate and unhappy.

She hates me. Martha could not keep this thought out. It circled her mind and came swooping in, plunging from the sky, when it found a way. It was a mad, stabbing thought! How could it be true? But it felt true, and with Clive gone to New York she could feel the shadow of that dark bird, *flick-flick-flicker*, as it passed over the house.

Val had eyed her with Eliza once and said, 'They're very unrewarding, babies. It's better when they get older.'

Clive had protested, 'How can you say that? Just *seeing* Eliza is rewarding.'

Martha held her tongue. She wished she possessed Clive's clarity of vision and, above all, his patience. He seemed to know everything about being a parent, and to find none of its duties dull.

He even seemed to know exactly what was wrong with his wife. 'You're not depressed about having a baby,' he told her, as firm and decided as a doctor tapping an X-ray with his pen. 'It's because of your dad.' As well as a diagnosis, he had a cure: 'Sell the cottage.' He said this once a month at least. 'It'll close that chapter. Then we can get a bigger flat, and you can get some help.'

Martha kept her temper with difficulty, for this was the flame which could set to blazes a full-blown argument: when Clive wanted to work, he got up and went to work; when Martha wanted to work, she was told she had to 'get some help' and pay for it herself.

'The cottage,' she said through gritted teeth, 'is worth more to me than a flat with a second bathroom.'

'Well,' Clive said, 'if you won't do that, then –' He spread his hands. *If you won't help yourself, then I can't help you.* Clive's gesture was as familiar as his argument – they both repeated these assertions to each other once a month.

Clive had gone, now, in a taxi to the airport. He had pulled a wheeled case from a cupboard, asking, 'Can I take this?'

Looking at it, Martha had recognised a suitcase that had once belonged to her. When she had worked, she had flown in and out of the country so often that the case had never gone back in the cupboard – putting it away and fetching it out had felt like too much of a hassle. Since it was always either being packed or unpacked, in those days, it had shared their bedroom with them, like a baby's cot.

From the sanctuary of his Manhattan hotel Clive stared out at the city which unrolled away from his window to the pale, winter's horizon. He had never been here before and here was everything: *New York*. He hovered in the air above a glorious, limitless, glittering planet, the same as his own and yet not.

He considered the wealth of his position: separated from wife and baby and with designated free time. *I can do anything I want.*

His imagination flared and died like a struck match. There was nothing he wanted; nothing he would do. He was obedient, cheap and reliable – it was why Belinda had brought him. 'Please,' Justin had begged, his forehead resting on the desk and his eyes closed, 'please. Do something bad, while you're there. Something you regret. Something to tell me about when you get back. Something. Anything.'

Behind Clive the hotel bedroom promised nothing: a bed tucked tight like a fancy napkin; a wipe-clean menu of television channels; a chained rail of coat hangers in an echoing closet. Pursed lips, clasped hands and a tight collar. Clive did not want to turn around and face it.

Instead he leaned his forehead on the window and placed one palm beside his face, the fingers spread, as if he were making a forlorn, farewell signal to a person on the sidewalk far below. He thought of Eliza.

That morning she had bumped from chair to table in the bedroom – tottering on two legs – fingers outstretched as if she were feeling her way to a light switch – and then pitched forwards and rumbled about on her hands and feet again. Clive wished he could take her everywhere with him and watch her, just for the pleasure of it. What would she be doing now? His heart tripped and recovered itself.

Belinda Easton, who was now in the room next door, had two children of her own but Clive knew no more than that – he did not know their names or their ages. She did not speak of family or friends, only work. Once Clive had asked how old her children were and she had replied, 'Enormous.'

Clive wondered what she was doing this minute while he stood with his hand on the window. Sleeping? He pictured a water glass on the bedside table and her plain face twitching as she slept. All at once he felt absurd; embarrassed; peculiar, and he thought of Justin. 'Mate,' Justin would have said, 'you're a dirty perv.'

In a flurry Clive remembered his duty: not to waste this precious time away from home. He emptied his bag on the bed and made a mess of the room – this was what Justin would have done – before taking a long shower, using all the towels and wrapping himself in a heavy robe. He pulled beer and snacks from the fridge and flung himself on to the hotel counterpane to stare at the television and finger the remote control. This would have been the moment, he noted, when Justin would have watched porn and had a wank but Clive turned – with another kind of shame – to the news channel and lay in a soggy cocoon of linen and litter until it was time for his meeting.

Sluggish and woozy he dragged himself off the bed and into his leaden clothes. He had eaten every snack in the minibar. Under his feet the carpet was a gravel of pistachio shells. In the bathroom he stepped into a puddle and cursed aloud. He heard a cough from the next-door bathroom: Belinda. He froze. She could hear his every movement and – what was worse – Clive could imagine hers. She might at this very moment be tucked up on the loo like a pixie, those famous tights bound around her knees and her face a concentrating triangle. He tiptoed from his bathroom. On the edge of the bed he slumped into a defeated half-moon, peeled off his socks and filled in a laundry slip. It was almost more than his brain could accomplish. When he straightened up he heard his vertebrae click like a rosary and the dirty maggot of a headache wriggled up his neck. He did not want to go to work; he wanted to go home.

Back in a taxi at the end of the day, Clive rehearsed the excuses he would use to get him out of a dinner-for-two with Belinda: headache, nausea, jet lag – the old favourites. He knew he was being cruel, but an upholstered booth in the hotel restaurant, piano tinkling in the corner, was an evening he could not face.

He might have been prepared to be persuaded into a drink, but he was not given the chance: Belinda turned to face him across the slippery seat of the cab and announced that she would be spending her evening alone. 'Room service, a bath and a movie on telly,' she said. 'That's what hotels are for.' She must have caught a glimpse of hurt in Clive's expression for she added, surprised, 'You don't mind, do you?'

'Of course not – I agree. I think I'll do the same.' Clive turned to look out of the window.

'You? Stay in?' Belinda teased him. 'Not likely. We all know what a *player* you are, Clive.' She was joking of course, and Clive laughed along.

Back in the hotel he wondered what he would do. It was too late to telephone home, but too early to cut his losses and go to bed. His room had been swept clean of wet towels, discarded food and detritus – to make a new impression he would have to repeat the solitary pantomime he had conducted earlier. He stood in the centre of the room and drank a cold beer from the fridge, wondering if perhaps he would go to bed after all. Neither Martha nor Justin need ever know.

The ring of the telephone gave him a fright. It was Belinda. 'These people are *paranoid*,' she said. 'Clive, can you run round to Lynton's suite at the Arcturus and fetch a bundle of stuff out of his safe? He doesn't trust a courier. It's only a matter of showing your face, picking it up and coming straight back.'

'Of course,' said Clive, untwisting the telephone cord with his free hand. Something to do! An errand. He swelled with self-importance.

'If you meet him, don't say anything – you'll make him nervous. Shake his hand and call him "sir" if you get the chance. I know it's ludicrous but this is the sort of thing they care about. When you get back I'll put the documents into the safe.'

Clive threw back his shoulders, walked nine blocks to the Arcturus and bowled up to reception feeling necessary and important. Placing both hands on the chest-high marble surface of the desk, he spoke to a manicured girl in a headset who looked straight through him until he had finished speaking and then said, 'Go on up,' and pointed to a lift, in the corner of the lobby, which served the penthouse suite alone. Once inside Clive checked his teeth in the mirror as red numbers flicked to sixty on a little dark screen.

After only a few seconds the doors opened – slowly; gingerly – to reveal not the usual hotel arrangement of landing, fire extinguisher and rubbish bin but instead a fully furnished room in which the elevator seemed to be both incongruous and incidental. Each marble-topped surface gleamed a different shade of mottled pink. Across the largest table a Prince tennis racquet was wrapped in a matt, black sheath and it seemed to point and stare at Clive until he quavered on the carpet. The lift doors remained open a moment, as if they too were encouraging him to return to the lobby where he belonged, and then with a sigh of resignation they slid together. Clive was left alone. He felt as if he had made the villain's entrance – from beneath the stage – and that his appearance would be met by jeers and catcalls.

The air and the carpet seemed both to be thicker up here, and Clive ploughed from one room to the next with the shuffling steps of a polar explorer. It was quiet, but for the distant sound of a television. He waded toward the noise through a kitchen, a scullery and a dining room – each more of a gap than a destination – and came to a halt in the chilled atmosphere of a gym, where CNN boomed at a cluster of petrified equipment.

Clive cursed himself and the machines before trailing a sorry path back to the lift. From the table the Prince racquet mocked him and he stood before it for a moment, penitent, before setting out again in a different direction. He traced another sound – the hysterical babble of a sports commentary – across a plush, puffed sitting room in which a shining black piano made a glossy puddle on the white carpet. Hurrying now – he must have been in this labyrinth for a thousand years – he approached an open doorway.

Before he could check his progress Clive had arrived in a bedroom. A roaring television hung on the wall and three huge men were perched on stools, looking up. Behind them stood an enormous bed and at its centre lay a quill-shaped man – narrow-shouldered and neat – with socked feet crossed and a celestial spread of pillows behind his head.

Knowing he had come too far, Clive teetered on the brink. Beyond the bed – beyond the window – lay the sparkling city, black and white at night. He imagined leaping out of this chamber and into the Milky Way.

The three spectators continued to stare at the screen with parted lips, as if about to receive communion, but the man on the bed stopped murmuring into the telephone and turned his head to stare at Clive.

This was Belinda's client, Lynton, recognisable from the profile Clive had read in the *Financial Times* ('*Gentleman – Yachtsman – Billionaire*') but also from his uniform – white sports socks and crisp white T-shirt; tracksuit trousers shaded the same expensive charcoal as his hair – which was standard leisurewear for billionaires and looked as if it had been bought at Saks today and delivered to the door of the bedroom in a fluttering nest of tissue. In a suit, Clive – like the seated thugs – could be identified as staff.

The laid-back pose was not convincing: Clive could tell that Lynton held in reserve the chilled athleticism of a leopard on a branch. With a flick of his tail, it was plain, he could be up and on you with his pointed teeth in the back of your neck. When he spoke – putting his hand over the receiver – it was in a tone of polite but lethal interest: 'And who the hell are you?'

The three men – perched in a row like circus sea lions –

turned their gaze from the screen, twitched at Clive and opened their mouths to bark.

Clive began, 'I'm –'

But then – 'Clive?'

It was a voice he knew, and he turned to face it. The city flickered beneath the window and the crowd bellowed from the television, but here in the room – half-dressed, half-dry, and halfway through hooking diamond earrings in her ears – stood Eliot Fox.

On the morning after Aiden's funeral, Clive had seen an otter. He had left Martha asleep in the cottage and gone for a run: into the woods behind the house, over the hill and along a track which took him down to a river. He had stopped to tie his lace beside a still, brimming pool, where branches hung their fingertips over the water and a lick of vapour skimmed away in a careless arabesque.

Straightening up, he had paused to look and taken in the perfect, balanced harmony of the moment. The water lay before him, its surface undisturbed: one chord would draw the ballerina from the wings to tiptoe a shy, tilted path towards centre stage.

Clive had felt like an intruder. The previous day's wake had been long, liquid and emotional; a tight, sticky residue of alcohol – whisky and champagne – still hung about him like a drift of tiny flies. He had held his hot breath rather than cloud the air.

As he stood motionless a smooth, drenched head had emerged from the water in front of him. Streaked in brown and tan, it was as clean and washed as a handful of stones on the riverbed.

Otter.

It had not seen him but had swum, frowned into the depths, turned about, dipped and ducked. A swirl – a loosely written circle on the surface – and it had gone. Clive had waited – hoping – and it had come again, slipping through the water like a knife through silk. It was light and strong; serious and laughing; thinking and instinctive – all these things were bound together and buttoned inside its tawny coat.

Clive had been astonished and had felt – with a flash of something near joy – as if his sins had been forgiven and that this sight was the proof: here was a blessing, swimming before him. He had thought of himself – *what I did* – and then of Eliot – *what I did to Eliot.* She had swum into his mind's eye – he had kept her out for so long, *why today?* – and he had wanted to weep, to fall to his knees, to grind dirt from the path into his eyes.

Why think of her? Because there was something of Eliot in that creature – rare, purposeful, tender, humorous – that worked as it played, and played as it worked. He had remembered Eliot's hands at the piano: swim, soar, dip, soothe, search. The privacy of that work which was play to her. He had begged out loud, 'Oh, please –', and the otter had heard him, looked and vanished.

Clive had finished the sentence in his head: *Oh, please let me begin again.*

Back at the cottage he had picked his way upstairs to the bedroom through the mess of empty bottles and glasses left by the funeral party. He had found Martha still sleeping, her face a slide of make-up pressed into the pillow and her black dress dropped on the floor. Clive had woken her up and asked her to marry him.

But this was the living, breathing Eliot, here in this room. Not a forgiving spirit but a towering, fearsome person, standing before him with the might to judge him still. Clive knew at once he had not been right to forgive himself that morning, standing beside the river. Here stood the girl who had written in her felt-tip pen, *I hate your guts and I hope you rot in hell.* Whether she hated him still was for her to decide for herself.

He had thought of her since that morning – of course he had – but only for as long as it took to spell her name out in his head: *El-i-ot.* At its closing consonant he repackaged the word and put it away.

He had not forgotten – he had neither forgotten nor remembered – until Martha, pregnant and explosive, had announced the name she wanted to give their daughter: Eliza. *E-l-i.* Clive had felt the clutch of the ghost at his arm and he had bent down to the floor – tying his shoelace, hiding his face, buying some time – before straightening up to reply. But what could he say? *No, not that name . . .*

'Why not?' Martha would have demanded. 'It was my mother's name, Clive. Why not?'

Because it reminds me of that girl we used to know . . .

*

111

Here she stood: *that girl.* He stood in front of her, turned to stone.

Eliot laughed. 'You look as if you'd seen a ghost!' and hearing the chime of her voice Clive thought, *Perhaps it is going to be all right.*

'Who is this guy?' asked Lynton. 'Friend of yours?'

'I know him.'

'What's he doing here?'

'I don't know.' She turned to Clive. 'What are you doing here?'

'I came for a document.'

'You're the guy? The barrister? From London?'

'That's right.'

'Small world,' Lynton said. His voice was chalky with distrust.

'You'll never guess how I know him,' Eliot said. 'It's such a funny story –' She was watching Clive who swallowed and cringed in terror like a thieving, cornered dog.

'Oh yeah?' queried Lynton.

Eliot waited a moment with half a smile on her lips and then she said, 'Never mind. I'll tell you another time.'

Clive wanted to dive through the glass and into the hooting metropolis but instead he licked his lips and tried to speak. 'I had no idea—' he began.

But Lynton spoke too. 'How did you—?'

Eliot interrupted them: 'Let's have a drink,' she said. 'Since you're here.'

She pulled a dress from the closet and slipped it on over her underwear, right there in the room. Clive and Lynton watched

112

her but the other men did not even turn their heads. Then Lynton glanced – cat-quick – at Clive and caught him staring.

'Come on,' Eliot beckoned Clive. He followed her into the next-door room which contained the piano and, he noticed now, a bar. The men stayed where they were. 'Lynton's team is playing,' Eliot explained. 'He wouldn't move if you set him on fire.'

Behind the bar, Eliot pulled open a fridge door. Bottles of champagne were arranged in neat rows and she lifted one out, stripped the foil from the neck of the bottle and twisted out the cork. She paid as little attention to the task as if she had been snapping open a can of Coke or squeezing a carton of milk.

Clive watched her, waiting for a cue. She was very thin under the black, clinging stretch of her dress. He noted the sharp prongs of her shoulders, elbows and pelvis; the mark of each rib as she turned to pluck two glasses from a high shelf. Her face by contrast seemed unstructured – as pale, featureless and distant as a winter moon. Her hair was short and bleached to white; even her lips and eyes seemed to have been washed of their colour. Most vivid were the glittering diamonds which swung to and fro below each ear.

Eliot did not ask him what he wanted, but pushed a glass of champagne towards him. She unwrapped a pack of cigarettes from a packet on the bar, and lit one. She did not come and sit next to him but stayed standing where she was.

He thought she might not say anything, and so he spoke. 'You don't seem surprised,' he said.

She exhaled a gust of smoke. 'I'm not. People always crop up again, in life. Didn't you imagine this would happen? I did.'

She had become sophisticated: Clive saw it in her dead-eyed look; he heard it in the flat tone of her voice. Nothing would be extraordinary; nothing would surprise her. 'Yes,' he said. 'I suppose I did.' He had imagined a chance meeting, but never a conversation – and certainly not this. He was unmoored. 'How are you?' he asked.

'Me? Great. Good. Brilliant, actually.'

'How long have you ...'

'Been with Lynton? For a bit.' She seemed to have smoked the whole cigarette already, and ground out the stub. She stared at the packet, scratching the back of one hand with the nails of the other. Clive could tell she wanted another one. He was thinking, *She can't be more than twenty-one.*

'So you're a barrister,' she said. 'You said you were going to be. How clever of you,' she gave a flat, mocking laugh, 'to have realised your ambition.' In a gesture that seemed to signify both defiance and surrender she took another cigarette and lit it before refilling both their glasses.

'I'm only a junior,' apologised Clive. 'Not much more than an assistant, really.'

'Oh, don't be so hard on yourself, Clive,' she said in a voice that fell like salt. 'And what else? Wife? Baby?'

'Yes.' Why did he not want to admit it? 'Both.'

'I knew it!' she exclaimed. 'Don't tell me: you married Martha?' She laughed even more when she saw from his face that she had guessed right. 'How did you manage that? Did you get her pregnant too?'

Clive was shocked, and he hated her – that bitter voice would spoil everything it spoke of. He thought of home, of

Eliza's face and the puff of her breath as she slept. 'We've got a daughter,' he admitted, reluctant.

'How sweet,' mocked Eliot, taking a glug at her drink. 'And what about Martha's ambition? I can't picture her as a house-wife.'

Clive flushed. 'She's fine,' he said. He waited a moment for the hot wash to ebb from his face and neck. Then he asked, 'What about you? What are you doing?'

She didn't say anything for a moment. 'Doing? I'm . . .' She looked around the room, as if for inspiration. 'I like music,' she said, eyes lighting on the piano.

'You always did.' Clive's voice seemed to leap at the posi-tive – at last he had been thrown a ball he could return. 'Do you remember, you played the piano in the hotel lobby in Normandy?'

She smiled and said, 'Did I? What a little brat I must have been. Well: now I've got my *own* piano in my *own* apartment. How about that?'

'Where?' asked Clive.

She looked at him. 'What do you mean, "where"? Here – right here in this room.'

'Oh, I thought you meant –' But he could not continue. *I thought you meant you had your own apartment; your own home. Anywhere but here.*

There was another pause and then Eliot asked, 'How's Tom?'

Clive did not want to tell her anything more, but his head hurt and he felt weakened by this awful torture. He might not want to speak, but he could not keep himself from talking. 'He's fine,' he replied. 'He's going to be a doctor, if you can believe it.'

'Yes, I can,' said Eliot. She had expected this too; she seemed to know everything. Clive quickly drank his champagne, blinking as he tipped the glass back. He noticed that in the ceiling above the bar little sparkling lights had been set so that there was something to look at when you drank.

'What are you doing tonight?' Eliot said next.

'Tonight?' Clive repeated, stupid and confused. 'Nothing. I mean ... no, nothing. Why? What time is it?'

'I've no idea. Does it matter? We're going to something,' she said, frowning, 'but I'm not sure what. Some "do", probably. Why don't you come?'

'I can't ...' But in fact, he could; he could not think of a reason why not. 'Well, I could I suppose. But it's a bit weird, isn't it? I mean, Lynton's my client.'

'Oh, don't worry about that; Lynton's adorable –'

Clive doubted this.

'– and in any case, you said yourself – you're only the assistant. It's not like you're the big silk who's going to get up and represent him in court.'

The way she put this point – which he himself had made – unnerved Clive still further. He was afraid.

'Come on,' went on Eliot, 'will you? For me?' She turned the lit end of her cigarette around in the ashtray. She looked down at it and then up at Clive from under her lashes. 'I'm so fucking lonely, Clive.' The words were a surprise – and she said them so quickly – he wondered whether he had heard her right.

'OK,' he said. 'Yes.' Guilt would make him do anything she asked, he realised, for eternity. He feared her; he was paralysed;

he could not run away. He would stand quite still and wait for the plunge of her knife between his ribs.

Eliot smiled her half-smile and said, 'I'll be back in a sec.'

In those days, if – when – Eliza woke in the night she cried with a loud, snagging, persistence that – although there was nothing wrong – did not stop. She did not have to be upset, hungry or uncomfortable. She might not even be awake. She might just cry, on and on.

Martha and Clive had different ideas about what to do. He would get up; she would not. 'If you leave her,' Martha would say, 'she'll stop.' But they never knew because they never did: Clive was always there, and Eliza was always nestled to sleep on his shoulder.

On that night – for the first time in Eliza's life – there was no Clive.

'What will you do?' he had asked, before he had left for the airport.

'Don't you trust me?' Martha had replied. To herself she had said, *I will not give in.*

When she woke up she lay in the dark and listened to those lonely, miserable sobs in the neighbouring room:

'*Uh-hic – hook – raawl . . . Uh-hic – hook – raawl . . .*'

Martha remembered the vow she had made to herself. She closed her ears. *I will break this habit,* she thought. *It will be an achievement.* She was determined. 'No, Eliza,' she said. 'Not this time.' She put a pillow on her head and fell asleep.

Waking from a tiring, rasping, clattering dream – something precious lost; something left undone – she heard the same noise, relentless, but louder and more urgent. Eliza had not stopped.

Oh God. That sound. Please, no more.

Martha switched on the light, looked at her watch and was frightened. She got out of bed, trembling a little and saying 'all right all right all right –' half to herself.

In the next-door room she stared into the cot. 'What do you want?' she asked. 'Tell me.' But Eliza did not even open her eyes to see, she just cried, and the stress of crying had turned her face to blotches. Now her legs shuddered and her fists beat on the mattress. Now her mouth was huge – huge – but not breathing, only yelling; now that sound was continuous, dreadful, inhuman: a yowl like a desperate cat.

'Hushushush – it's OK –' With a snatching, worried movement Martha plucked Eliza from the cot and cuddled her to her chest. Why had she not done this before? She cursed herself and folded her daughter into her arms but it seemed to be too late: Eliza did not understand – or believe – that this was rescue, fighting her tormenter as if she were struggling out of a knotted sack. She wriggled and pummelled, kicked and screamed. *Oh*, Martha begged her, mute, *please stop*. Tears filled her eyes and she felt both their hearts pounding, loud and fast, frantic and feverish. Pressed together like this their fractious tussle was gathering pace and Martha could see no end – she could not make it stop and Eliza did not know how.

And then: *milk*. The idea came into her head and she swept Eliza upstairs. She put her down on the kitchen rug and knelt before her. 'Please,' she begged aloud, 'stop. Please –' but Eliza took no notice, turning her head from side to side and yelling.

Martha sat back on her heels. Watching this angry, twisting creature she wondered, fearful, *What are you?*

Once this monstrous thought was let loose it disturbed others – panic, rage and terror – which tumbled from Martha like angry wasps. *Shut up shut up!* The fear which she could bat away by day – *Eliza hates me* – hovered and droned about her head and she could not seem to frighten it off. From this fear grew a sulky distemper and then a resentment which seemed to spread like a vile, toxic mould. *I should have left you lying there,* she thought. *It makes no difference what I do.*

She felt an icy detachment. Standing up, she switched on the kettle and turned to the fridge. *Milk.* But what was the point? Nothing she did would satisfy Eliza. This crying was like an alarm going off in the street: at first it drew attention – people came out of their houses and wondered who to tell – and then all the front doors were shut, and life went on as before. The noise stopped in the end.

She thought she might make tea for herself but she fumbled and dropped a mug. Picking up the two pieces – handle; cup – she noticed her hand was shaking. She turned to Eliza: *See what you've done to me?*

Eliza struggled for breath – '*Hook-hook-hook*' – and the kettle murmured and puttered on the counter.

'Oh, Eliza, please,' Martha begged, 'please.' She knelt on the rug and repeated it over and over; a monotone, a prayer, a chant. The blue light from the kettle glowed and lit them from above. 'Please, Eliza, please.' But Eliza did not stop.

119

There's something wrong. There must be.

Martha sat back on her heels again. Damn Clive! 'All right,' she said, 'you win. We'll phone your dad.'

The word alone had an immediate effect. To Martha's relief – and dismay – Eliza continued to wriggle and gasp but she switched off her yelling at once. She turned her head and quizzed the room. Martha could see the question in her face: *Where is he?*

Feeling quite hollow inside, Martha got to her feet. Eliza lay curling and hiccupping on the floor while she searched for the number of Clive's hotel. When Eliza began to mewl again, Martha exclaimed, 'Oh fuck – oh God –' She checked herself and took a deep breath. Now she saw it: a large yellow note on the wall with the words 'New York' and a number. Clive had stuck it to the wall where she could find it in a moment, if she needed to. But now where was the telephone? Nestling among the cushions of the sofa in the next-door room.

'No reply, ma'am.' The hotel receptionist was brusque.

'What? Not in his room? Are you sure?' Martha looked at her watch. *Where was he?* In the kitchen behind her the kettle rumbled itself off, and now she heard the effortful puffs of Eliza, on the floor and gathering breath.

From New York: 'Would you like to leave a message? Ma'am?'

'What?' Martha turned her head back to the telephone. 'Oh, let me think –' A message. Did she want to leave one?

But then she heard something else – just a very innocent noise.

'Ma'am? Do you want' –

120

A small, surprised sound – as if someone had thrown a cushion which had struck the wall. Nothing more than that.

– 'to leave a message? Hello?'

What was that?

But Martha knew. She took the receiver away from her ear and turned around with a cold, cold feeling – realisation; acknowledgement – pouring over her body.

Eliot left Clive sitting alone at the bar for much longer than 'a sec'. When she came back she had changed her clothes and he pictured her undressing and dressing in front of those men. 'Don't you mind having so many people in your bedroom?' he asked.

'Which people?' she replied. 'Oh, them. No, I don't give a shit, actually. You get used to staff.'

She had painted her face to go out for the evening: red lips and blackened lashes. Clive thought of the wet, streaked head of the untroubled otter. How stupid he had been – there was nothing of that creature in the tall, sinister being which stood in front of him now.

Staring at her Clive wondered what had happened to her army jacket and the little bee that Tom had given her. Because he had now drunk most of the bottle of champagne, he asked her.

'That?' She gave another of her tin-can laughs. 'God knows. Junked, probably. Sent to *charidy*' – she mocked a New Jersey accent – 'to help the *paw baby awphans*.' She rattled again with laughter. Everything made her laugh, but nothing was funny at all.

'Listen,' she went on. 'Update: Lynton's got some meeting downstairs so we can have another drink up here which is good 'cause I can smoke. Shall I make Martinis' – her eyes gleamed – 'or are you worried about your job? Always fretting about something, aren't you, Clive? What a little worrier you always were. Here's something to *really* worry about: Lynton thinks you're weird, says he thought you were a pervert, coming into the bedroom like that. But I told him, "He's not a creep, babe! He's one of the good guys! You can trust him! I've known him since I was just a little kid …" Lynton's got kids, he's got a daughter at boarding school … weird, huh? "Pleeze *pleeze*, babe," I said to him, "can't a girl hang out with the first guy she ever got screwed by, for old time's sake?" Just kidding, Clive – don't look so freaked out! As if I would.'

Clive's ears were being assaulted by the *ack-ack-ack* of her voice.

'He's a softie really,' she babbled on, 'Lynton I mean. He wants me to go to the Juilliard or the Conservatory, one of those places. Ha! He's *vewy* sup*paw*tive' – she put on her joke voice again – 'which is nice, huh? So anyway he said you can stay and keep me company 'til he's done.' She touched the back of her hand to the tip of her nose and teetered on her heels.

'Really? No, I mean, look – listen –' said Clive, scared and helpless, 'I think maybe I should just go –' He edged off the stool, wishing he had not already drunk that champagne.

The phone behind the bar began to ring but Eliot just raised her voice to speak above it. 'No way! You're not going any-fucking-where.' She pushed his shoulder with a sharp finger, and Clive sat back down. Slapping her tiny handbag – a flat,

122

green, lizard-skin envelope – on the bar, she flipped it open. 'Whaddya wanna do,' she said. 'Make drinks, or make lines?'

'Neither,' said Clive. 'I don't—'

'Fucking square; you always were. Open another bottle, I'll do this.'

Clive got up and went behind the bar; he would use the time to think. He pulled a bottle from the fridge and began to open it. The telephone began to plead with them again, over and over. Eliot took no notice, busy with her coke. 'D'you know,' she said, 'I always wanted a Platinum Amex. It's nice when you get what you want, huh? Don'tcha think?'

As Clive stripped the foil from the neck of the bottle he said, 'I thought you didn't do drugs?'

This seemed to be the funniest joke so far. When she had stopped laughing she said, 'Well, Clive,' in her most chatty, confiding tone. She wiped the edge of the credit card and rubbed her finger on her gums before continuing. 'You know you're right –' she wagged the finger at him – 'and it's a *funny ole story* because I didn't use to, and then something made me start. Hm.' Now she put her finger beside her cheek, pretending to think it over. 'I wonder what that was?' With a cackle she rolled up a twenty-dollar bill, stuck one end in a nostril and snorted up the line with a long, reaching breath. Then she licked her finger, wiped it over the glossy surface of the bar and rubbed her gums again. She watched her reflection in the mirror behind Clive and put her head on one side. 'I look like a whore,' she said in a matter-of-fact voice. The phone began to bleep again, its red light flashing.

Clive said nothing. He thought he might be feeling sick.

Concentrating hard, he thumbed the cork from the champagne bottle, poured a glass for Eliot and said, 'I'm going for a pee.' After opening and shutting several doors he found a bathroom and locked himself into it.

Reeling, exhaling, he sat down on the lip of the bath and shut his eyes. When he opened them it was to find that every surface of the bathroom, including the floor and ceiling, was covered by a terrifying black marble which meant that he could not be sure he faced the right way up.

He would unlock the door, walk out of the room, out of the suite, into the lift, back to his hotel and go to bed. In the morning he would telephone his wife. That's what would happen next.

In his wallet was a picture of Eliza. 'Hello,' he whispered, pressing the tip of his forefinger to the photograph. He knew he was drunk.

He came out of the bathroom and went back into the sitting room. Standing in the doorway – he did not dare go closer – he said, 'I'm leaving.'

She was as prepared for this as she was for everything. 'Well, fuck you,' she said in a flat tone. Then she swivelled round on the stool to face him and bared her teeth to say, 'Joke – that was a *joke*. Jeez. Hey, wait –' she swept the detritus – card, note, coke, cigarettes, lighter – from the bar into her handbag, slid off the stool and on to her feet – 'I'll come down with you.'

She did not say anything else and they waited for the lift in silence, the Prince racquet pointing its accusing finger at them from the table.

In the lift, Eliot scratched at the back of one hand, over and over. Clive heard a voice say, 'Eliot,' and it was his own. He had not meant to speak, but now he could not help himself. 'I don't want to leave you here. Not like this.'

Eliot looked at him. For a second she did seem surprised, but then she caught up with herself and blanked her expression again.

'What can I do to help?' Clive went on. 'I want to help—'

'Help? Help?' She mocked him and turned away.

Clive was silenced; he did not know what this meant.

Staring straight ahead of herself at the closed lift doors Eliot said in a bored voice – as if she had been saying *I'll have the tuna on rye* – 'What do you think this is, Oliver fucking Twist? Do I look like a ten-year-old kid? You've got a fucking nerve, Clive. "Help"?' She laughed. 'I wouldn't even be here without you.'

Clive watched the red numbers on the screen, *flick flick flick*, count back down towards the lobby. *5 – 4 – 3 – 2*.

'Fuck you,' repeated Eliot, punching the button to open the door, 'and fuck your precious life. You don't deserve it.'

When the lift doors slid apart she seemed already to be moving – half out and walking away from him – *tack-tack-tack* across the shining white floor.

Clive stood still.

A voice said his name, 'Clive?' Now Belinda was standing in front of him, wearing a coat and tracksuit. Her tired, white face seemed to have lost its structure.

Clive stepped out of the lift – its doors were trying to close – and towards her. What was she doing here? 'Belinda?' Then he remembered his errand. 'I forgot the file.'

'That doesn't matter,' Belinda said. She held out both hands in a placating gesture which frightened him. 'I've been trying to ring but I couldn't get an answer – I was on my way up. Your wife has phoned.' Her voice was – what was the word for that tone? – *grave*. 'There's been –' her mouth closed and opened – 'an accident. Eliza's hit her head. I've booked you on to a flight –'

She continued to speak, and Clive watched her lips move. The word that had been repeating in his head – like a running heartbeat – changed shape:

Eliot Eliot Eliot
Eliza Eliza Eliza.

Waiting for his flight at JFK, Clive told Belinda about Eliot. 'I expect you're wondering who that girl was,' Clive said, 'the one in the lift.'

'Not really,' Belinda replied, 'but it sounds like you're going to tell me.'

Clive told her everything. It was in part to fill the dead time they had to sit through; in part to distract himself from the crisis that waited in London; in part because of that emergency, and in part because he wanted to hear that none of this was his fault.

When he stopped talking Belinda blew air out of her cheeks and stared down at her shoes. Then she said, 'I don't know why you think she's worse off here with Lynton than she was with you.' She sounded tired and depressed.

Clive had not expected this and he did not – could not – reply. His surprise must have shown in his expression because

Belinda continued, 'Well: think about it – at least he cares where she is and what she's doing; at least someone will notice if she doesn't make it home one night. It sounds like you and her parents – between you – did a pretty thorough job of fucking her up.' She stared into Clive's face which had turned the stained grey of an old dishcloth. 'What do you want me to say, Clive? That it's OK? That you didn't do a bad thing? Were you expecting sympathy?'

Yes. Please.

'Well, tough. I've got a fifteen-year-old daughter at home. I wish you hadn't told me any of that. It's a bad, rotten deed, what you did. If I were Martha and I found out, I'd—' She stopped and started again. 'I don't know what she'd do if she knew.'

The mention of Martha chilled Clive but seemed to refresh Belinda, to give her back a sense of purpose, and she peered up at the winking screen – *Departures* – above their heads. In a different tone of voice – one that had been washed and dried – she said, 'The only thing that matters now is Eliza. Let's not mention it again.'

Once on the plane and stowed in his window seat Clive began to regret his confession. He had not been prepared for the harshness of that judgement – Belinda had condemned him in a bold and indelible type. It had been foolish to tell her.

The plane pressed forward and lifted into the air; Clive wrestled with his terrors. Everything but Eliza was trivial: *forget Eliot*. But try as he might he could not dismiss from his mind that wretched other girl, the shock of her words and the swim of the falling lift.

His mind raced as the plane made its steep ascent. Belinda had told him to put Eliot out of his mind, and that was what Clive must do: *forget it.* To afford Eliot even a corner of his concern – given the circumstances – would be unspeakable. He would not – could not – think of anyone but Eliza. He spoke to himself with a voice of authority: *Eliot's present situation is neither your fault nor your responsibility.* Her accusations had been disproportionate and – yes – more than that: unjust.

The aeroplane relaxed its climb by a few degrees, and Clive settled more comfortably in his seat. He looked out of the little oval window beside him and remembered what Eliot had said in the penthouse, before she had taken the coke: *Me? Great. Good. Brilliant.* When she used those words to describe herself, there could be no need for concern.

Outside the window the lights of the city were nothing but dwindling points. Clive pulled down the blind and looked ahead at row upon row of quiet, placid passengers. His near environment was calm, and now the cabin was brightened again as they levelled off. He was reminded not to smoke, advised to keep his seatbelt fastened and implored to press the bell if he needed attention. Obedient, relaxed, Clive let his shoulders fall into the seat. The plane struck out across the lightless span of ocean towards home.

8

In her hospital bed, Eliza lay mute and inert – a butterfly pinned to a card – but the room was not quite silent: *mip-mip-mip*. In the past, Clive had listened out for her sleeping breath. Now he heard this.

Martha sat beside her, knotting and pleating her hands.

'Come home,' Clive pleaded.

'No.' She was stubborn; white-faced; resolute. 'I'm not leaving her. Never again.' She was as good as her word.

Belinda sent flowers to the hospital: *For you both at this difficult time.*

When it was safe to take Eliza home, Clive brought her and Martha – strapped and reluctant – back with him in the car. He felt like a kidnapper: Martha sat next to Eliza, Eliza yelled and Martha cried too, as wordless as her daughter. They clutched each other's hands. Clive watched them in the mirror as he waited at every set of red lights. He could think of no words to comfort.

Martha did not make it easy: 'I wish we could stay in hospital for ever,' she said that night. She stood staring into the cot and pulling at her lips with her teeth until she made them bleed.

'Let me help,' Clive begged, but she would not answer. She fetched the camp bed and slept – lay awake – in Eliza's room.

In the morning, Clive went to work and the other two stayed in the flat. It was just as it had been before – it was the same routine – and yet this time it had nothing to do with Clive. Martha came into her own, and Clive was no longer useful. Eliza was undamaged – 'It's little short of a miracle,' they were told – but now she was out of his reach.

Home became clean, quiet and tidy. Frustration and anger vanished overnight, along with smoking and the snapping bad temper. Both gates on the stairs were kept shut, and Martha and Clive scissored over them. Precautions were taken against other types of accident: smoke alarms appeared, kitchen knives were locked in a cupboard, a safety catch was fixed to the dishwasher door, windows were barred, outdoor shoes banished and surfaces polished with antibacterial cleanser.

Martha's time was spent in the pursuit of domestic excellence. She did not mention the past, complain about the present or articulate a future of any kind. She took to homemaking with the zeal of a religious convert: the flat sparkled, Eliza and Clive glowed, their clothes shuddered round in the washing machine and the kitchen shelves were piled with cookery books.

Clive, back from work, would try to find his place. 'Can I help?', he might ask.

Martha would look up – from the sink, the hob, the bath or the bedtime story – and reply, 'No; don't worry; it's all done.'

Can I help?

No; don't worry.

At weekends Clive felt unwelcome – an accessory. 'What's Daddy going to do today?' Martha would ask Eliza on Saturday mornings. She did not want him there, she wanted Eliza to herself. Clive's presence alone was a disruption to ordinary service – Martha described Mondays as, 'Getting back to normal'.

Disconsolate, Clive began to spend Saturdays at work but there was not always work to be done, so he joined a gym and went there. Sometimes he stayed, after he had exercised, to drink a freshly made juice and read the weekend papers.

He asked Martha when she would like to go back to work.

'Work?' She blinked at him.

On another day he asked her, 'What about getting some help?'

'Help? What for?'

'So that you ... can have some time to yourself. Away from Eliza.'

'That's not what I want.' The subject was closed, and the days and the months went by.

*

Clive knew what had happened, and he knew why: *Fuck your precious life. You don't deserve it.*

He knew that Eliza would never remember her father holding her bottle, upturned toward her besotted gaze, in their quiet London kitchen. While he would remember sprinkling water on her in the bath, she would not. He would always know that to pluck and *swoosh* her from the cot had made her laugh, but she was too young to remember it into the future. That precious life had been captured and placed behind glass; pinned to a card with its wings outstretched.

Part IV

9

The cottage was nothing to do with Clive, and that was how it felt. Standing beside it tonight, watching his taxi grumble away down the stony track that crossed the field to the lane, he felt a familiar mood settle on his shoulder like a shuffling, black-feathered bird.

Martha often referred to her cottage as 'Dad's'. When she did, Eliza would say, 'Can't we call it something else? "Dad" means *my* dad, not your dad. Your dad's been dead for ages and ages.' She had never known Aiden and spoke of him with careless disregard, but she was even more haphazard with Martha's mother. 'The deadest of all is your mum,' she occasionally intoned. 'Not even you remember her.' It was true: Martha had been too small to commit her mother to memory. 'It's like Dad says,' Eliza comforted her, 'you can't miss what you never had.'

Dead relations were not interesting, but the consequences were. 'You're an orphan,' she would say to her mother in a voice both pitying and envious. 'Like Harry Potter and Oliver Twist.'

'All the best children are,' Martha would tease. 'I bet you can't wait to get rid of us!' It was one of their favourite jokes.

Clive was not here alone – Martha and Eliza must be about somewhere – but he felt it. There seemed to be nothing moving but the steady drip of water from the leaves. Claws gripped his shoulder: *loneliness*. A roosting bird; black head tucked under black wing.

He glanced at the fretwork of the holly tree, a sharp silhouette against the moth-soft evening sky. This tree stood sentry in the garden, breathing and wakeful, while the others blurred and rustled in a wood behind the house.

Clive had wanted to cut the holly down but the man who came advised against it. 'It's bad luck to cut them down.'

'But it makes the house dark.'

Martha had scented reprieve. 'Just leave it, Clive, will you? Let's not tempt fate.'

When he had begun to earn decent money Clive had wanted to do up the house. He had told Martha that if he was going to have to spend every weekend there he wanted be comfortable, but in fact – he had acknowledged this only to himself – he had wished to repay Aiden for that sneering put down: *Commercial law? Your bank manager will be very proud.* There would be an achievement, however sordid and private, in renovating Aiden's house on the proceeds of the very career he had sniffed at.

Clive was denied the satisfaction, however, because Martha attached such sentiment to the house that she would not let him touch it – he did not seem to have any rights whether Aiden was dead or alive.

Exasperated, Clive had said, 'Fine: keep it; pay for it.' She had taken him at his word.

'My work, my money, my cottage,' she would tell Clive when he tried to interfere. 'You can be the boss in London.'

Martha's devotion to the cottage did not need superstitions to keep it alive, but she embraced them when they came: 'It's a lady holly,' she had reported. 'They have berries. They guard against evil spirits – that's what the tree man said.'

You're everything my father's not, Martha had said once and Clive, hearing what he wanted, had melted away for the love of her.

Aiden would have put it another way: *I am everything you're not.*

Aiden had died in this house alone, and Martha had found his body. It was thought – by the village doctor – that dying must have taken him a little while. It had been another little while before he was discovered.

Clive could be superstitious too. He turned his reluctant stare up to the roof. *Bats.* Right away – although he could neither see nor hear them – he thought he could sense their feverish, snickering presence, teeming and trembling, up in the rafters.

He began to picture them, chattering and diabolical, a

wriggling, soil-brown knot that burrowed in the dark. Now he could smell the greasy mash of their fur, see the folds of flaccid skin and hear the click of spillikin bone.

'But Dad, they're sweet,' Eliza had said, puzzled. 'Look.' She had shown him a photograph on the computer screen. 'They've always been there. The only difference is that now we know.'

The only difference; all the difference. Clive stepped up to the front door.

He walked in to find Martha halfway downstairs and picking cobwebs off her jumper. 'Oh – you're here,' she said. 'Did it rain in London? It poured all the way down the motorway.' She was in her own cottage mood: present but absent. 'I've just been in the attic,' she went on, 'looking for those bats and their babies. It's stifling up there, but apparently that's what they like.' To herself she said, 'I must take all that stuff to the tip some time.' It was something Clive heard once a year.

'Where's Eliza?' Clive asked. The house did not feel as if there were another living person in it.

'Ah,' Martha said, guilty and smiling, 'when I tell you, don't freak out –'

Clive felt a tremor. He knew what was coming. It was an approaching train and he was strapped to the rails. *I am not surprised,* he thought. *I have no right to be surprised.* The train would come and cut him in three: head, body and wriggling legs.

'– there's no point; it's done now and you'll only ruin our evening together.' Martha fiddled with her watch strap and then looked at him and said, 'I let Eliza go with Eliot.' Now she took another step towards him. She would come close enough for a kiss, with the idea that it could placate him. 'I'd already said yes. I couldn't tell her no – not without a reason. She was so excited; Eliot's her friend.'

Tell Martha? I won't have to.

Clive had pictured this scene – oh, a thousand times – but he had never rehearsed the actual words he might use. Now he groped for them, staring with a blank face at his wife. How, he wondered, could something so familiar to his mind be so impossible to communicate? It was unspeakable; unsayable. Whatever words he used the meaning would not translate. He would be unintelligible. He was not equipped with the skills or the tools that he needed.

Martha read his expression – frightened; struggling – and her own face changed. 'What is it?'

'There is a reason.' These were words; it was a beginning. There was a pause, as if he had dropped four stones down a well and was waiting to hear them splash.

Martha said again, 'What is it?'

He had never imagined what might appear in Martha's face as he told her. Now he watched as every word she heard made a mark and coloured it in until her expression was so terrible – hurt; shock; rage; fear – that he could not bear to look at it. 'I slept with Eliot,' he was saying, 'years ago. That's why I didn't want – I don't want – to be around her.'

Martha was about to speak – he felt the air tense and thicken – and so he hurried on – *Yes, there's more*.

'She . . . I got her pregnant.' He stopped. Swallowed. Started again. 'She had an abortion.' Now he shut his mouth.

Martha let loose a word that darted away like a swift: 'When?'

His speech was so slow, it slid from his mouth like paste. 'When we were doing our finals.'

'Our *finals?*' Now she stopped; now she started. 'So she was ... at school?' Thinking, calculating, she looked past him and out of the window.

Clive stepped forward.

'Don't come near me,' Martha snapped. 'Get back. Let me think.'

He waited. Every moment he grew more transparent and Martha turned more opaque. When she spoke again she seemed almost made of stone. 'I want to see her,' she said, 'I want to see them both. Let me past.' She faced him, from her higher step.

'Martha –' Now it was Clive's turn to try to placate.

'Let me *past* –' She stepped to the floor and roughly pushed him with both hands, forcing him aside. He felt her meaning and gave way, shocked, to that message: *Let me past, you brute.* She picked up her car keys from the shelf beside the door, and said, 'You wait here. Stay here.'

'Please—'

'*Stay here!*' She turned and shouted it at him – as if she would have hit him with her fist, if she could – and then she had flung out of the door and was gone.

Martha knocked on Eliot's front door and when it opened she said – as quick as a slap – 'Where is she?'

'Martha! What are you—?'

'Please! Eliot! Let me see her.'

Now Eliot looked at her again and said, 'So you know.'

'Yes of course I fucking know. Let me in.'

Eliot opened the door and Martha blew in and up the stairs in a gust. Upstairs she found Eliza asleep in one half of Eliot's bed.

Martha exhaled a long breath. She stood looking down at Eliza, wanting to wake her but knowing it would not be sensible – it would only alarm her. 'OK,' she said. 'OK.' She let her shoulders drop and her hands unclench.

Downstairs in the hall again, Eliot said, 'Are you all right?'

Martha looked at her, unseeing. 'I don't know,' she said. 'I can't take it in.' Then she asked, 'Have you got anything to drink?'

In the kitchen a bottle of brandy, expensive and ribboned, stood on a high shelf. 'What about this?' Eliot reached up to fetch it.

'That'll do,' said Martha. She drank, held out her glass and drank again. Eliot fetched a stool and Martha sank on to it, shoulders hunched and feet tucked underneath. As the alcohol took hold, fear loosened its grip. Now a rage – a churning, sulphurous heat – spread from her insides out. She turned her glass, as heavy as a paperweight, in her hand. She had not yet decided at whom to aim her anger or her punishment.

Eliot, watching her, stood with her back to the dark square of the kitchen window and spoke, as she did of herself, in tied-up portions. 'When I met Eliza at the school,' she said, 'I didn't

141

know what to do.' She paused. 'I always thought I'd see you again one day – it was inevitable – but not in such . . . ' She stopped, searched Martha's face and changed tack. 'I realised,' she continued, 'as soon as I saw you, that Clive had never . . . ' Another pause. 'It wasn't up to me tell you.'

Martha listened, but none of this seemed to be what mattered now. Her mind was turning back to face her past – her history – both near and distant. Recent days, weeks and months were lit by insight and then the years before, each and every one of them, began to be illuminated too. A sun was rising over a landscape she had crossed in darkness, and only now did she see how treacherous her journey had been. Every marker, turning point and resting post in her life was now spotlit by brilliant daylight. Nothing was what it had seemed.

'It changes everything,' she whispered. 'It touches everything.' Wishing it might not be true, she tried to say, 'But it's impossible. Clive—'

'– would never do something like that?' Eliot's words struck Martha's out of the air. Now Martha knew it was true, and now she believed it.

Clive opened his eyes and saw in front of him a cold, swept fireplace. He was on the sofa in the cottage, dressed in his clothes and lying under a blanket. He stayed still for several minutes.

He felt quite different this morning – not like a new man, but like a ghost of the old one. The Clive of yesterday had vanished for ever. That man had come clean, and wiped himself out of existence.

With a groan and a thud, he rolled on to the floor and lay

on his back, pegged to the rug by invisible ties. After a few minutes he felt the ground around him with his fingers. *Telephone*. When he found it he checked the screen, but it was blank. 'Leave a message for Martha,' said the cool instruction when he rang her number. He did not wait for the beep.

He could call Tom, but – he blenched – *not quite yet*. Martha would have told him, he was certain, on her way to London last night.

With that conversation playing in his head Clive could not stay on the floor. He pulled himself to his feet and stood looking out of the window. *This house. I can't stand it. I won't stay.* He rang for a taxi, shut the front door and went back to London.

Eliza woke at Eliot's house. She felt an excited lurch inside and rolled over – but here on the bed was not Eliot but her mother, perched on the corner beside her feet and looking out of the window at the sky.

'There's only my bed,' Eliot had said to Eliza on the way home from the concert. 'We'll have to share.'

'I won't sleep anyway,' Eliza had replied. She had been so happy she wanted never to sleep but to go on with this feeling for ever. She had come straight upstairs from the front door and brushed her teeth with Eliot's toothpaste, in the bathroom where Eliot's washbag lay by the sink and her towel hung over the rail. It was strange to think of someone as special as Eliot drying her face with a towel like everyone else.

Eliza had climbed into the side of the bed where there was no bedside lamp. 'My side,' she had said, wriggling down. Eliot had kissed her goodnight – 'I'll be back in a minute' – and gone back downstairs. But despite her intention Eliza had fallen asleep right away, and had missed the treat of sharing.

Now Eliza was confused. 'Mum?' she said. She sat up and pushed her hair out of her eyes.

Martha twisted around to face her. 'Hello, pet.' She smiled, but only a small amount.

Eliza did not smile. She frowned. 'What are you doing here? Where's Eliot?'

'Downstairs.'

'Where's Dad?'

'In the cottage.'

'Did you have an argument?' This was said in a voice that implied, 'Really, you two are the living end.'

Martha looked at her. 'Sort of.'

'Was it about me and the concert?'

'Not you, no. The concert a bit.'

Eliza was practical. 'How did you get here?'

'In the car. It was late. I came to talk to Eliot, and then I sat in the car for a bit, and now I'm here with you.'

'But that means no sleep at all!' It was baffling. 'Were you drunk?'

'No! Of course not.' They looked at each other, and then Martha smiled, this time with a bit more meaning. 'How was the concert?'

'Oh, Mum.' The thought of it drove everything else from Eliza's head. 'Amazing. Literally amazing. And we had ice-creams in the interval *and* we got a taxi back. But you know what, Mum' – now Eliza put her head on one side – 'I might want to learn an orchestral instrument. They're more *sociable* than the piano.'

Her mother looked at her. 'That's a good word,' she said. 'Did Eliot suggest it?'

'Yes,' admitted Eliza. 'But I agree with her.'

'So do I. Sociable is nice.'

'Yes, and playing the piano is a bit lonely sometimes – Eliot says – because there's no one next to you.' Eliza's hands drifted over an imaginary keyboard on the duvet in front of her. 'I was watching the people in the orchestra and they were all ... friends, you know? Smiling and winking and things. I bet it's fun – I could be like that.'

Having made her speech, Eliza was embarrassed. She rolled forward on to her head on the bed until her pyjama-striped bottom pointed up into the air.

This was Martha's cue to reach around and pull Eliza's feet over her head until she was lying flat again on the mattress, gig-gling. It was an old routine. 'That sounds sensible,' said Martha. 'Come on then, maestro: breakfast.'

It should have been nice, having her mother there in the morning, but it was not. Three was not as good as two, and Eliot no longer belonged to Eliza. There was no talk of the con-cert or of the promised breakfast in the café. Eliot said nothing at all, and Martha was hungover – Eliza could tell by the turned-down look of her mouth and eyes – which meant tired and cross. Eliza wished her mother had stayed away. 'What was so bad about the argument that you had to come here?' she asked, peevish. 'Why couldn't you have stayed with Dad? We were coming anyway.'

'Stop it, will you?' Martha said in irritation. 'Anyone would think you weren't pleased to see me.'

This was met with a speaking silence.

Then it got worse: 'There's been a change of plan,' Martha said. 'Eliot's not coming with us to the cottage. We're going on our own.'

Eliza wanted to cry. 'Why?' she asked.

'Stop asking questions. Just because.'

Yesterday Eliza had imagined sitting in the passenger seat of Eliot's two-seater, sharing a Twix and discussing *The Carnival of the Animals*. Today she and her mother drove in silence, the windows up and the radio off.

It was traditional for Eliza to jump out of the car and race up the field to the cottage but today, when they arrived, she did not feel like it. 'Why not?' Martha tried to make her.

'Why should I?' said Eliza.

'You always do.' They sat in the stationary car, the engine running.

'Not today.' She was stubborn; it was an impasse.

'Fine.' Martha accelerated in a skid of stones.

Up at the house they both looked out for Clive but there was no sign of him. 'Where the fuck is he?' Martha said under her breath.

Eliza shrank at the swearword and the spitting anger in her mother's voice. This was not right. She got out of the car and ran inside, shouting, 'Dad?', but it was more to get away than anything else. She searched the house and found nothing different except a blanket on the sofa where it should not have been. She looked at it with a strange feeling growing like mould on her insides.

In the kitchen Martha was standing, doing nothing. 'He's not here,' Eliza said, walking back into the room.

'I know.'

'Where is he?'

'I don't know. At home, probably.'

'What's going on, Mum?'

'Nothing. Why don't you go for a walk?'

'I don't want to. I wish I was in London with Eliot. It's boring here and you're being horrible.'

Martha seemed to collapse like a burst paper bag. 'I know,' she said. 'I'm sorry.' She chewed on her next words before she came out with them. 'It's complicated.'

Now Eliza felt guilty. 'We could make a cake?' she offered. 'Or watch a film?'

Martha smiled a very sad smile. 'Yes,' she said. 'Let's.' But they both heard a car on the track and swung to the window to see who it was.

'Dad?' queried Eliza, her voice a hopeful treble.

'Tom,' said Martha, looking at the car. 'Tom –' And she sank into a chair and started crying out loud – very loud – in a burst of tears with her face puckered into her fists.

By the time Tom walked into the kitchen Eliza was patting

her mother's shoulder with a light, tapping hand that begged for help as much as it sought to comfort. Her expression made a worried, white disc of the face that she turned towards Tom.

The flat was empty and had not been visited. Clive stared down at the mute, white covers of his bed. *Our bed*, he tried to reassure himself. *The bed I share with my wife.*

Next he stood in the kitchen, wondering, and looking at the washing-up in the rack. This place did not feel like home – but then nor had the cottage. Where could he go? He thought of his mother.

'You!' she said when he telephoned, stuffing the word with meaning until it seemed to burst on his ear like a flung cushion. 'I thought it would be you. I've just had Tom on the phone. What a mess!'

Clive did not say anything.

'Do you know, Clive, if you weren't my son I don't think I would be able to forgive you.' She paused, as if hoping that he would feel at the mercy of such a fate. But the moment did not last long – the jeopardy did not convince – and she spoke next with a mother's resignation. 'I suppose you want to come here,' she said. 'I don't know where else you can go.'

Tom was like a cowboy crossed with an astronaut, Eliza often thought, but perhaps that was because of the car he drove. It was called a Space Wagon and the name spoke to her of starry nights, camp fires and rockets to the moon.

He needed a wagon, he said, because of his two sons. He

said what he would like best would be a wagon he could pull behind him like a pony pulls a cart, because then he would not have to listen to the shouting and fighting.

Sometimes he teased his boys, saying, 'If only I'd had twin girls! Two lovely girls with pigtails!' It made the boys roar and blush.

Stan and Jack were younger than Eliza by two-and-three-quarter years but they seemed to take up at least as much room as she did. Their real names were Stanislaus and Jascha because their mother, Kathy, was Bulgarian. 'But they've never even *been* there,' Eliza had said when she first learned this. 'They don't even *speak* Bulgarian.'

'Kathy does, and her parents do,' Tom had replied. 'Don't be such a bossy boots, and give me back those passports.'

Eliza did not like being told off by Tom and so had left the conversation there, but she bore a grudge. She was not sure with whom. Kathy? She knew that she wanted England to be more important to Stan and Jack than Bulgaria because she wanted them to belong to her family. She did not have brothers and sisters, two of her grandparents were dead and one had moved to France – she needed every remaining relation she could find. For Christmas and birthdays in particular.

Tom used to live with Kathy and the boys, but now he worked in a different hospital from hers and lived in another flat, only seeing them at weekends. This did not satisfy Eliza. 'Don't you miss them?'

'I don't have time,' Tom had said, and it was bound to be true because he worked so hard.

Tom was a doctor, 'With a particular interest in children's

brains.' When he said this to Eliza he wiggled his fingers like Doctor Frankenstein. It was a private joke between them because of the time she had fallen on her head. '*Donk-donk-donk*,' he would say to her, rolling his eyes. 'Do I hear the sound of Eliza coming downstairs?'

Anyone else making jokes about it would not have been funny but with Tom it was always all right. To be teased by him was not a punishment – it was more like a blessing. This particular joke, however, had to be a secret. It was not the sort that Martha or Clive would find funny. 'But soon I'll be a surgeon,' Tom whispered to her. 'Then you can fall down the stairs as much as you like, and I'll just stick you back together.' Eliza giggled.

Eliza could not miss having siblings because, as her father often said, 'You can't miss what you never had.' But after her cousins had left – at the end of a half-term or a holiday – the cottage did feel very quiet. Cleaning her teeth on her own (and not being spat on or shoved out of the way) was not as nice as she remembered.

There was always a moment, however, when they first faced each other that she stared at the boys, and they at her, as if they had never met. This time was the same: Mum went to the bathroom to blow her nose, Tom got three Ribenas out from the cupboard, and the children stared at each other like fish in a bowl. 'Out,' said Tom to them. 'And don't come back.' He meant until tea, and he held the kitchen door open for them until they had shuffled out into the yard. Eliza wanted to stay – *What about Dad?* – but the door was shut in her face and once

150

she was outside it did not seem to concern her. Now there was a simpler matter at hand: the field, the stream or the camp in the woods?

Jack said, 'Let's make a dam –'

'– And then a flood,' finished Stan.

'Race you,' said Eliza, and off they went.

In photographs her cousins looked alike, but when they were running about or speaking they were Stan and Jack, and not identical at all. Tom had once given her mother and father a telling-off for calling them 'the twins'. 'Please don't,' he had said.

'Not even to you?' Martha had not really understood him.

'Call them by their names, like you would anyone else.'

Eliza had understood him perfectly – but then, she had not needed to be told. 'It's like when Dad calls you "my wife",' she had chipped in, trying to be helpful. 'You don't like that.'

'Eliza, I wish you wouldn't interrupt grown-up conversations,' her mother had said, turning in her chair with a cross face.

That night Tom shouted in the garden, in the dark. Martha had gone to bed with a crash – too much wine again – but Tom liked to smoke outside and Eliza, who was awake, heard the click of the front door and smelled his tobacco. Smoke had a habit, Eliza had noticed, of creeping indoors – like spiders did before thunderstorms. She wrinkled her nose.

Now she heard him speaking. 'You fucker,' she heard. She could hardly believe her ears. This was horrible. Was it even

Tom? He had a different voice, like stamping on a cardboard box. 'How could you?' These pauses meant he must be on his telephone. 'How could you do it to Martha? To Eliot?' (*Eliot?* frowned Eliza in bed. *But what—?*) 'And to me, you bastard, you knew how I felt . . . '

Eliza got up, with her heart leaping arpeggios in her chest. She shut the window without making any noise, put on her iPod and – back in bed – turned out the light. Music in the dark was better than hearing . . . *that*. This was a moment for *The Well-Tempered Clavier*, which made her think of Eliot and of the previous evening when, in the Albert Hall, everything had been not just all right but wonderful, marvellous, special and perfect. It seemed long ago and far away from here.

In the flat on Sunday night there was no sign of Clive. He had been there – his running shoes, toothbrush and laptop were gone – but he had not slept in the bed. Eliza stood at the door of her parents' bedroom and looked at the smooth, flat duvet which – like the blanket strewn on the sofa in the cottage – told her only that something was wrong. Her wondering imagination reached and roamed all over, looking for answers. The peculiar feeling inside was not going away but spreading, staining her bones, turning her green like old cheese in the fridge. She imagined the gradual rotting and spotting of her ribs and her fingers, under the skin.

Upstairs in the kitchen she was nervous of her mother and did not say anything. They had not spoken much today. Tom had made sausages and mash for lunch and Martha had sat and stared at nothing in particular, drinking red wine and pulling at a hole in her cardigan. She had stayed in the same position when her food was put in front of her, and then she had not eaten it. When she had asked Tom for one of his cigarettes Eliza had been courageous and said, 'Please, Mum, don't.' Her mother had not even replied, just gone ahead and smoked. In the car they had not spoken at all. Eliza had put on *Just William*, but only to drown out the silence.

She waited, standing in the kitchen with her rucksack, to find out what would happen next. Martha shuffled through the letters and then opened and shut the fridge door. 'Ugh,' she said. 'How depressing.'

Eliza had an idea. 'Why don't we ask Eliot to come over? And bring pizzas? We could watch a film.'

'No.' It came out in a snap, but then Martha took a deep breath and said, 'Not tonight.'

So they ate cereal in their pyjamas and watched something about lions, and Martha cried when the lioness attacked the baby elephant. This was normal – Mum always cried in nature programmes – but what followed was not: she continued to cry for a long time afterwards, right up until the end. It made Eliza nervous. 'Come on, Mum,' she said, patting her. 'It's not that sad, it's just what lions do: she's got to feed her family group. It's like pizzas for them.'

'I know,' said Martha, trying to smile and squeeze Eliza's patting fingers on her shoulder. 'I'm fine. A bit tired, that's all.'

But this was not 'a bit tired', Eliza knew. She wanted Dad, Eliot or Tom to come and help. 'Mum,' she began.

'Please Eliza, no more questions.' It was the voice which said, 'You are trying my patience.'

After brushing her teeth Eliza snarled and roared at herself in the bathroom mirror. 'We're a family group,' she said. 'You and me and Dad.' She thought her mother might need reminding of something good.

But Martha – who was folding up towels in slow motion, as if each one was incredibly heavy – put her face in the one she held and started to cry again. 'What about Eliot?' she asked. 'What about her family group?'

'Eliot's not a lion,' said Eliza, turning round in surprise. 'She's a tiger – she goes around on her own.'

Now Martha sat on the edge of the bath and smoothed the folded towel on her lap with both hands. In a slow voice she said, 'Eliza, we're not going to see Eliot again.'

'What?' It was like ice cubes thrown in her face. 'Why not?'

'Because . . . oh, *God*, it's impossible to tell you. I can't. But you'll just have to accept it.'

Martha was angry and tired, but Eliza was angry too. 'What about the piano? I'm still doing that, aren't I?'

'No.' Silence. Then, 'You said yourself you wanted to do another instrument.'

'But . . . I meant *as well*.' This was not fair. That was not what she had said. Eliza frowned. She wanted to cry, but also to throw her toothbrush at the wall. Crying won. 'Please don't do that, Mum,' she begged. 'Eliot's my friend and I love the piano, you know I do.'

'Eliza, stop it. I feel bad enough as it is—'

'Well now I feel bad too!' It was a shout and a blur. The toothbrush skidded into the sink and Eliza was gone from the room.

The next day Clive was standing outside the school when Eliza came dragging out through the gate with her rucksack bumping on the ground behind her. He smiled. 'Well?' he said.

Eliza looked up. 'Dad Dad Dad,' she said and brimmed with relief. They held hands and walked to the park. 'Where have you been?' she asked him. It was all going to be all right.

'I'm visiting Mum. Your granny.'

'Visiting? What, still? Why? Is she ill?'

'No. I just . . . felt like it.'

Why did no one answer her questions? Eliza wondered. Everything she asked got a reply but not an answer. If she had said, 'Because I felt like it', she would have been told off.

'Without us?'

Clive said nothing to this at first and then, 'For the moment.'

This was bad. It had been nice to see him, but this was rotten. Eliza was no fool: 'Dad, you've got to make it up with Mum,' she said. 'This isn't . . . it's not . . . ' She struggled to describe it.

'Come on,' he said, getting up. 'I said I'd get you back for tea.'

But Eliza did not get up. 'No. Tell me you'll make it up.'

'I'll try.'

'No, Dad.' She pulled his hand. 'You've got to actually do it.'

They walked home but he would not come in even though she tried to drag him. She dropped his hand, then, and climbed the steps on her own without turning round. On each step she said, 'Pig,' under her breath.

Martha was waiting for her in the kitchen. 'Oh, pet –' she said when she saw Eliza's face, and put out her arms.

'Go away,' shouted Eliza, in a furious kicking rage. 'You don't get to hug me.' She ran down to her bedroom and slammed the door. When she looked out of her window and up to the pavement her father had gone.

10

Clive had gone to meet Eliza because Martha had sent him a message: *Collect Eliza from school pls. Get her back here by 5.* He had stared at the instruction, as formal as a summons, and felt sorrow give way to resentment, seething inside him. He had simmered through the rest of the day and then gone to the school gates.

'Get used to it,' Belinda said the next morning. 'That's what life is like for divorced fathers: written instructions and penalties if you disobey.'

'Rubbish,' said Clive, quelling the flutter of panic. 'And anyway, we're not getting divorced. Martha just needs time.'

'She needs an apology,' said Belinda in her sharp way.

'I don't understand why you're angry with me too,' complained Clive.

'Because' – she was so eager to tell him she bit his question off – 'you never should have got away with your shitty, awful behaviour and now you have to pay for it. You deserve this, Clive. You don't need better representation, you need to plead guilty. Don't you get it?'

Perhaps I don't, Clive thought with a doleful – but somehow delicious – resignation. *Perhaps I only know the letter of the law. Perhaps I am amoral.* It was a tempting thought: everything beyond his control. He was confused and needy. 'Are we friends?' he asked.

'Friends?' Belinda was nonplussed. She did not seem to recognise the word.

Clive put his query another way: 'Do you hate me, because of what I did?'

'I hate what you did,' Belinda said. 'And I wish you were sorry for doing it.'

'But I am.'

'No you're not,' she rebuked him. 'You're only sorry because you're frightened of losing your family. You're sorry for yourself.'

Yes I am, Clive thought. *What other way is there?* 'Sorry' would always start and end with himself.

Clive's bedroom, in his mother's house, had been swept clean of childhood belongings and turned into a spare – a musty bottle of Highland Spring stood beside the bed. Tom's room had not been redecorated since he had spent his adolescence there, and Clive apologised for it to Eliza. 'But I like it,' she said, dumping her rucksack on the bed. 'It reminds me of Tom and that's nice.'

Clive was not consoled by this reaction. He grumbled to his mother, 'Tom's room is like a shrine.'

Val did not hear him. She was worried and wearing a knitted face. 'I think this trouble has hit Eliza very hard,' she said. 'She's angry. With you and her mother. She doesn't know what it's about.'

'Thank God,' said Clive, alarmed. It was bad enough his mother knowing.

'I expect you blame me, do you?' his mother said. 'Men usually blame their mothers when they do something horrible.' She was pulling no punches, at the moment. Clive accepted it as the penalty for living in her house.

Val lived alone because she and Peter had, as she said, 'Parted company.' She liked this description because it closed a door that opened when people asked her whether she was married. It seemed to satisfy them – she supposed because of her age – and it was accurate. She and Peter had been companions, but now they were apart.

It had not hurt to lose him but to live alone had been hard at first – not lonely, but difficult. Bills, insurance premiums, car maintenance, the garden, buying wine, her bank account, people who came to the door or rang her up out of the blue. But she had learned it all – so satisfying! – and now it was easy, even the internet. She could eat snacks and not meals, and watch what she wanted on television without being asked, 'What else is on?' The lawn grew tousled – she did not care for neat, mown stripes and never had – and the shrubs grew tall and stout. She went more often to London, and took her time in the supermarket.

She had been surprised by how little the separation had affected her. Even when Peter took up with an English lady in France – 'Dad's got himself a bit of stuff,' Tom had joked – she had tested her heart and found it not torn but springing and intact. 'We led such different lives,' she had told herself, feeling a touch of guilt. 'It was a long time coming.'

She knew she would mind much more if, say, Tom were to move out of London (the thought lifted tears to her eyes) or Martha and Clive were to split up. This latter idea, conjured up at random over the years, had become a sudden and present dread because attached to it came the greater terror: that Eliza would be taken away to live with her mother abroad.

Martha – with her translating work – could be carried off who knew where. 'Anywhere from Laayoune to Muscat,' she had boasted once, long ago, and Val had pursed her lips when she had found those places on the map.

Then there had been that kerfuffle over the United Nations. 'New York?' Val had queried Clive. 'But what about you? You can't be a barrister in America, can you?'

'Of course not, Mum,' Clive had said. 'I'd have to give it up, or not go.'

'What are you going to do?'

'I don't know. We haven't talked about it. Martha's away.'

'She's always away.'

'She likes to work.'

Val had dreaded the telephone call which would answer her question, *What are you going to do?* But it never came. The next time Clive rang it was to say that Aiden had died.

Eliza was angry. She loved Granny Val – Gravel – and being with her was normal and fine. But Dad was worse than nothing, at the moment. He was like someone ill, or old. He sat in a chair and said, 'What?' whenever she asked him a question.

'Just like his father,' Val said. It did not sound like a compliment.

Eliza could only remember two things about her grandfather: his ears – enormous – had been clogged with yellow stuff, and he had always kept a Terry's Chocolate Orange in a secret cupboard. It had emerged, segment by segment, to reward good behaviour, but now that Grumpeter lived in France the cupboard was unlocked and empty.

'Why did he go?' Eliza had asked her mother.

'Well . . . he always liked that funny little town.'

At Val's house Eliza found Tom's diary, the one he had written when he had been a teenager and in love with Eliot. She could not put it down – nothing had ever been so fascinating. Reading it late into the night tired her out and during the day her head buzzed with Tom: Tom at school, Tom and his friends, Tom and Eliot: *'I love her. I'll never love anyone else.'* He had kept writing until Eliot had stopped speaking to him – he had not known why – and then he had trailed off and stopped.

I love Eliot too, thought Eliza. The story thrilled her and she yearned for *Chapter 2: A Happy Reunion*. Perhaps she could arrange it. She fantasised scenarios in which Tom and Eliot were together, happy and grateful. Perhaps they would ask her to live with them. She would practise the piano whenever she wanted and go to a different school. She would play in an orchestra, Eliot would teach and at home they would play duets.

After the weekend, despite knowing it had been forbidden, Eliza went to the music room and raised her hand to tap on the closed door. She could hear the piano and she knew it was Bach – the music which connected her to Eliot like a thread – but her nerve failed. She could not knock. She stood there, frozen, with one hand lifted and her breath making a furry disc of vapour on the glossy black paint. Perhaps Eliot would sense she was there and come out? Eliza waited, hoping, but the door remained shut.

In the playground before going home Eliot saw her and came up. 'Your parents don't want me teaching you anymore,' she said. She made it sound simple and clear, standing in front of Eliza with her music books folded in her arms. She was wearing a denim shirt that she wore often. 'It's because of something that happened before you were born. It's not your fault.'

'It's not fair.'

'No, it's not.'

This made Eliza feel better; peaceful. 'You must really like that shirt. I like it too,' she said.

Eliot smiled, which was rare and therefore precious. 'Listen,' she said, 'I had an idea: why don't you sing in the musical?

Then we can see each other in rehearsals. You could be a "work-house boy". It's like a chorus.'

Eliza shook her head. 'Too scary.'

'No, not too scary. I promise.'

Eliza paused and curled her toes as if she were at the edge of the swimming pool. 'Maybe.'

The musical was *Oliver!*. Eliot played a rippling chord at the beginning of the first rehearsal and said, 'Everyone should do *Oliver!* once in their life.'

'Did you, Miss Fox?' someone piped up.

'Yes I did, a hundred million years ago when I was at school. Now,' she went on, 'I want this to be fun, but I also want it to be *good*, and that means we've all got to try our best.'

Eliza was to play a hungry orphan at the beginning and a 'barrow boy', whatever that might be, at the end. Both required rags, bare feet and a smudged face, which meant that costume and make-up would be easy.

Now that she had a secret of her own Eliza bought a diary – 'Mum, can we stop at the shop on the way home? Can you lend me three pounds ninety-nine?' – and wrote everything in it: rehearsal times, Eliot's clothes, what had made everyone laugh, what was easy and what was difficult. She was surprised by how much there was to write. When she thought it over, after putting the lid on the pen and switching out her light, she knew she had been enjoying herself. This was like being in an orchestra: sociable.

'Are you an orphan, like Mum?' Eliza had stayed behind at the end of the rehearsal to help gather up the music from the floor, where everyone had dropped it. Now she sat down next to Eliot on the bench at the piano and traced her fingers over the keys.

Eliot took the score off the bracket in front of them and said, 'No. My parents are alive but . . . we've lost touch.'

'How come?' Eliza lifted her hands off the piano keys and sat on her fingers.

'Well,' said Eliot, 'I had a brother and when he was very small – and I was even smaller – he got ill and died.'

'Was it cancer?' asked Eliza. She knew about cancer – everyone did.

'A tumour in his brain. So my parents were pretty sad. Anyway later on, when I was a bit older than you, I got into trouble.'

'At school?'

'At home and then at school. One thing went wrong and then everything did. I failed all my exams and I ran away – I even stopped playing the piano. Mum and Dad got fed up. They said I had "wasted my opportunities"' – here she put on the deep voice of an angry father, 'and they kept having to give me money.'

'What for?'

'That's what they said!' It was not an answer, but Eliot went on. 'They told me to go away and leave them alone. So I did.' She had been looking down at the keyboard and wiping specks of invisible dust off the keys with her sleeve. Now that she had finished speaking she turned to face Eliza.

'And that's it?' Eliza drank it all in. 'That's really sad.' In a dreamy voice she said, 'If only Tom had been there.' The words fell out of her mouth before she could stop them.

Eliot looked at her. 'What do you mean?' she asked in a surprised voice.

'Oh – because he likes brains. Children's brains.' Eliza explained herself hastily. 'He could have saved your brother-who-died.'

Eliot smiled a faint smile. 'He was called Hector.' She paused and put her fingers above the keys as if she might play a chord, but she did not. Her fingers hovered and trembled a little at their tips. Then she said, 'Yes – I wish Tom had been there.'

'If it happened now, he would save Hector.' Eliza was keen to sing Tom's praises. 'He knows how.'

Eliot said nothing.

'I love Tom,' hinted Eliza, her voice heavy with meaning.

But Eliot said only, 'I bet you do, and I bet he loves you. How could he not? You're so completely-utterly-totally loveable.' It was said in a singsong voice and was sort-of a joke but Eliza, ecstatic, hung her head and let the words throb in her ears. She was too delighted even to respond.

They were both quiet for a minute, sitting quite still and looking at the keyboard in front of them.

Eliza tried to gather her wits. All this new information, heaped at the door of her brain! It seemed a chaotic, unmanageable jumble and to think of it made her feel breathless and light like a blown leaf. She wanted to slip off the stool and lie curled up on the floor but she knew there was work to be done and that these humming thoughts would have to be sorted, ordered and tidied away.

The prospect was intimidating: her head might bulge or

burst at the seams. Now it occurred to Eliza that a tumour would be the likely result of an overstuffed, disorderly brain. At once this idea seemed probable and her eyes widened in dismay. Heads were fragile – this much she knew for certain because Hector's had been and so was hers: *donk-donk-donk*.

She gazed at the piano keys in front of her and lifted her hands to rest beside Eliot's on the keyboard. Her own fingers looked small and hopeless by comparison. She thought of Johann Sebastian Bach: he could have made something harmonious from the swarm of ideas which had hatched and taken flight inside her head. She wished she possessed his skill; without it the bump and drone of trapped, unanswered questions – connected but nonsensical – would turn to a blur and then a feverish, tumultuous roar. It would batter her ears: *What of the past, near and distant? What of the future?* She would be overwhelmed.

'There are *millions* of notes in the world.' She stuttered the words in a desperate voice. 'It's too many. How am I supposed to manage?' She felt herself begin to wobble from the inside out; she wondered if this would be the beginning of a new, frightening and ungovernable experience.

But then Eliot turned to face her. She took Eliza's hands and clasped them in her own, holding Eliza above the swell of this swallowing sea. She looked straight into Eliza's questing, worrying face and said, 'It's going to be all right. It will be.'

Eliza did not want to argue; she wanted to be told. Right away her churning, tumbling thoughts calmed to a simmer as if she had been taken off the hob. Her heart slowed to its normal speed and settled to its usual place. Now she felt tears come flooding up from somewhere deep below – they would spill from her eyes in a flood, she knew they would. Her throat tightened and prickled in readiness; her forehead pinched and her mouth began to tremble. There was nothing she could do to keep herself in check, and she could not even hide her face for her hands were still held by Eliot's. She went limp, hung her head and waited for the torrent.

Eliot went on speaking in a steady voice: 'Not everything is fair,' she said. 'Some things are hard and horrible – like this thing you've got now, with your Mum and Dad: it's not fair and it's not your fault, but there's nothing you can do about it. You can't figure it out and you can't stop it. You just have to live with it, for a bit. But I promise you: it will be all right. I completely-utterly-totally promise.'

Instead of lying on the floor Eliza curled herself into Eliot's arms. She stayed there until the tears – every tear in the universe, it felt like – had all come out.

Eliza enjoyed rehearsals as long as she did not have to speak to anyone, and no one spoke to her. She had perfected the art of going unnoticed – it had taken years of practice. Being left alone was preferable to being singled out. Anything was.

There were two performances of *Oliver!*. Martha came to the first, and Clive to the second. Sometimes it seemed to Eliza as if the whole school was timetabled for parents who were not speaking to each other.

'When did you decide to sing in the musical?' Martha asked on the way home. She smiled as if she were pleased, but Eliza could tell she was not. 'Was it your idea?'

Eliza considered her answer. If she said 'yes' it would be a lie, but 'no' would get her into trouble – and probably Eliot too. 'You stopped me from having piano lessons,' she squeezed out after a moment, 'but not from *everything*.' It was the kind of artful, dodging conversation she was not used to having with her mother.

The second performance was on the last day of term. Eliza expected her usual ecstatic relief – *No more school for weeks!* – but this time it did not come. She had learned that school was just a place, and that people everywhere were sometimes nice and sometimes nasty. Even grown-ups, out in the wild, and even parents.

After the show everyone was elated, hugging and cheering on the stage behind the fallen curtain. Her father took her out for pizzas and in the restaurant loo she caught sight of her reflection in the mirror: an unfamiliar, glowing person – although still a bit smudged from the make-up – looked back at her. She almost didn't recognise herself. She pranced about for a moment singing *'Food* glorious *food* –' and then put her head under the hand dryer for a blow dry.

Back at the table her father tried to be cheerful but Eliza knew he was faking it. He ordered a Diablo, just like normal, and this time Eliza forsook her Margherita and had the same. She wanted to tell him something and this was a way, but it was not so nice and she had to pick the hot bits off.

Afterwards she was dropped off at home and she felt as if she were back in the playground with a sick feeling and a lump in her chest. She cried in the hallway and said to Martha, 'I hate it here!'

Martha said, 'Do you want to go to Granny's with Dad, for the night?'

'I hate it there too!'

In the morning she lay in bed, staring at the ceiling and picking at the corners of her fingers, peeling them away from her fingernails. She had not done this for ages – since before the piano. She could not do it and play because of the plasters, but that did not matter now.

At breakfast, when she was eating her cereal, her mother grabbed one of her hands. She looked at it, asked to see the other and then sat down next to Eliza at the table. She was still holding Eliza's fingers in her own, which made Eliza think of Eliot and want to start crying again.

'What about we all go to the cottage?' Martha searched Eliza's face. 'You and me and Tom and the boys?'

'And Dad?'

'Eliza . . .'

'I don't want to go without Dad. He's not *dead*, you know.'

This was enough to make Martha consider. 'All right. I'll ask him.' Eliza slumped in relief but now her mother began something new. 'So guess what?'

Eliza stared at her. *What now? Will it hurt?*

'I've got an interview for a job.'

This was not like having her hands held, it was like being cut open with a knife and then prodded with a fork. Eliza slipped her fingers out from her mother's grasp. 'A job?' she said. 'But you've got one.'

'No, a real all-day one, not a mum's one. Isn't that exciting?'

Eliza did not answer because she could not. She had the breathless, weak feeling she got in the swimming pool, halfway down a length of backstroke and veering off course. She had not known before today that 'exciting' could mean bad as well as good.

11

In fact it was Tom who told Clive about the holiday. Martha asked him to make the telephone call.

'We're all going to the cottage. Martha too. I've got the time off, and I'm bringing Stan and Jack.'

Clive ransacked his brain for excuses. 'But . . . ' he bleated, 'the bats. And then there's work. It's not possible –'

Tom might have said something in reply like, 'Oh grow up, will you?' But a bus hooted behind him at that moment and the words – whatever they had been – were lost. 'Just sort it out,' he went on, short-fused. 'Believe me, the last thing Martha or I want to do is spend time with you. This is for Eliza.'

Faced with this, Clive could not refuse.

He came off the telephone and went back into the kitchen where his mother sat at the table with her newspaper.

Val liked to read the newspaper first. 'It's not the same once you've pulled it to pieces. Can't you get your own? At the station?' But Clive did not want his own, he wanted his mother's.

Depending on his mood he might delay his commute, waiting for her to finish reading, and then take the paper from the kitchen table. 'You've read it,' he would bully her when she protested. 'Who reads a newspaper twice?'

Today would be one of those days. Clive was wounded, and he wanted to wound in return. He went over to the kettle and switched it on. 'I'm going to go to the cottage,' he said. 'Tomorrow. For the weekend.'

'To talk to Martha?'

'Sort of. We're all going. It's for Eliza's sake.'

'Good.'

But Clive had not finished. 'Tom seems to think that Martha is looking for a job, instead of working freelance.'

'Well, that's good too. She's often complained about wasting her brain.'

'It might be in Paris, Tom thinks.' Delivering this bombshell gave Clive a lick of satisfaction and then a sour taste.

Val began to turn the pages of her newspaper faster and faster until she had reached the back page when she pushed the whole thing away from herself and sat back in her seat. 'You can take that, now, if you want it,' she said. Her voice was neither kind nor unkind, but empty. Although she did not like to argue with Clive – he was too skilful and it sapped her strength – Val knew how to make herself plain. After a pause she cleared her throat and asked, 'Are you making one cup of tea? For yourself?'

It was Clive's policy not to respond to the most ridiculous of his mother's questions and this was one: the answer was staring her in the face.

'There's a pot, you see,' Val said. 'A teapot. It's for when more than one person might want tea. It's just more . . . *sociable*, I suppose.' She pursed her lips and spent a second or two arranging the salt and pepper cruets on the table. Then she continued, 'I think after this holiday you had better look for somewhere to live. If you don't sort things out with Martha, that is.'

Clive stirred milk into his mug of tea, making a whirlpool with his rotating teaspoon and causing the tea to slop at the lip of the cup. *Even my own mother.* He was stung. Behind his eyebrows a horde of venomous thoughts amassed, ready to retaliate. *Shut up, you bloody old woman.* Afraid to say anything – in case he said everything – he merely chinked his teaspoon twice against the rim of the mug, and laid it on the scarred wooden counter. Now there was quiet in the room and the only noise – the surge of blood and fury – came from inside his head.

But after a moment or two he was taken aback: he glimpsed, from the corner of his eye, a tissue flutter from Val's handbag and up to her face. They came one by one, like hatching butterflies, and he knew she was crying.

Martha took possession of the moral advantage and made good use of it, forging ahead with her desires.

'Every memory I have is spoiled,' she said to Tom. 'I need to take care of my future.' She was almost delirious with self-righteousness.

Tom had been listening to this, and to other versions of it, for an hour. He was subdued. 'You know,' he said, 'once a broken bone has knitted, it ought to be used. You'd be surprised,' he went on, looking out of the window, 'how often people go on limping longer than they need.'

Martha pretended not to have heard him. 'I want to work. I don't owe Clive a bloody thing. All these years I've been trying to make up for –' she swallowed, 'well, you know what. And all the time –' her tone grew triumphant '– his rotten secret! I want to go back to before. I want to start again.'

'All this "I",' protested Tom. 'There's Eliza too, remember?'

Martha was surprised and annoyed. She did not need reminding of Eliza.

It occurred to her, waiting to be petted in the delicious snug of the hairdresser's chair, that as well as gaining a new career she might fall in love and have another baby. *I might meet someone else*, she thought as she leafed through a magazine. *This happens to couples all the time.*

Val telephoned. 'Eliza is very angry,' she said. 'She's not herself. You must be careful, Martha, and not be selfish.'

'Selfish? Careful? Me? Your son, in case you'd forgotten—'

'I'm not talking about Clive, I'm talking about Eliza,' Val said.

Martha had never heard Val so assertive and it made her panicky. The hairdresser was poised, comb and dryer in hand. 'I can't hear you,' Martha said into the phone, indicating with her free hand that she was finishing the conversation. 'You're breaking up.' Now the dryer roared beside her ear.

*

174

Eliza travelled to the cottage by Space Wagon with her two cousins, her uncle and her father. 'I'll come after my interview,' Martha had said. Eliza did not want to hear that word, and she had not wished her mother luck when asked.

'You come in the front next to me,' Tom said to Eliza when they set off. 'I like a bit of civilised company up top.'

'What about Dad?'

'He can go in the back.'

It was a long journey and a tiring one – what with all the noise – but at last they reached the turning from the lane on to the track and there at the top sat the cottage, settled in its place like a bird on a nest. Tom stopped the car and said, 'Right, who's running?' The boys jumped out and were off like scudding rabbits across the grass. 'You?' Tom turned to Eliza.

'No, thanks.'

'Wise old lady,' Tom said, driving on up the drive.

Tom had only said one thing to his brother since they had left London, and that had been at the petrol station. 'I want to make a phone call, Clive,' he had said, looking in the rear-view mirror. 'Will you fill up the car?'

Tom had paced about on the grass where the litter bins were, speaking into the phone and kicking at a Coke can with one foot. Her father had filled the tank and gone into the shop to pay.

Eliza had never been to the cottage without Martha. It was like walking into the wardrobe where her mother's clothes were hung: private and somehow protecting. She had sometimes

175

spent Sunday afternoons hiding in that cupboard, sitting cross-legged on the floor with the dresses and coats dangling over her head, peeling her fingers and worrying about school the next day. When she had been very small and ignorant she had wondered if there might be a hole at the back of the wardrobe and a magical world beyond. Now she knew those worlds did not exist.

In the house Tom poured tea into mugs, and Eliza added milk. They listened to the weather forecast, which was for wind and rain, and Tom said, 'Excellent,' and rubbed his hands together. After tea he put up two tents on the lawn and ordered Stan and Jack into one. 'Go on, then: in you get. You wanted to go camping.'

'But Dad –'

'You said –'

'Somewhere *nice*.'

'This is nice.'

Stan and Jack were not convinced. They sulked and stared at their father with fishy faces. 'This holiday's rubbish.'

Clive was embarrassed but Tom was not. 'Hard cheese,' he said. 'We're staying here. You're sharing that one, and me and Uncle Clive are in the other—'

'I am *not*,' Clive expostulated.

'—and if he snores like a pig, I'm coming in with you two.'

This idea caused uproarious laughter from both boys who got into their tent to make pig-like snoring noises. Jack poked his head out and asked, 'Like that?'

'Yes, like that.'

From inside the tent Stan said, 'Dad, can we do whatever we want?'

'Pretty much,' said Tom. To him a camping trip meant no washing, bathing, brushing of teeth or regular meals. 'No fires, no explosions and no broken arms or legs, please. See how long you can go,' he suggested, 'without coming into the house.'

Eliza did not want to join in and muck about with her cousins. She did not want to stoop her way into their bitter-smelling tent. She felt too old and stiff for children's games. 'My head hurts,' she said when they asked her to play – it was an old trick she had not resorted to for years.

She spent the afternoon in her bedroom, writing her diary and listening to her iPod. Every few minutes she thought she heard her mother's car and took off her headphones to listen but no, it was always the wind. Hearing it moan under the eaves, rattle the window and shuffle the holly tree outside made her sadder and more lonely than she thought she had ever been. She turned up her music and cried.

Loud knocking at the door woke her up. 'Can you give me a hand? Please? I'm making supper for us and your mum.' It was Tom.

Eliza was groggy. 'Isn't she here? When's she coming?'

'Before supper I hope.'

'Where's Dad?'

'Gone to the shop. He took Stan and Jack, for his sins.' This was said in an amused tone of voice.

Eliza got out of bed and stumbled downstairs. In the kitchen she stood next to Tom and pricked sausages while he cut up potatoes – very fast – for mash. 'I may only know how to cook one thing,' he joked, 'but see how handy I am with a knife?'

He was referring to brain surgery but Eliza was not in the mood to play along. 'You're not a surgeon yet,' she said in a cold voice. 'You might not even get to be one. You have to be *amazing* to be one. You don't have to be amazing to cook sausages and mash.'

'Quite right,' said Tom and went back to his chopping.

Eliza felt horrible. Crying and sleeping had made her weak; now she was so weak she started crying again. She frowned, trying to stop, but tears splashed on to the sausages.

Tom passed a roll of kitchen paper to her and she mopped her face. When she had finished Tom said, 'Did you know I used to know your friend Eliot?'

Eliza nodded, not trusting herself to speak.

'She was my best friend, at school – when I was a bit older than you.'

'What was she like?' Eliza managed to stutter it out.

'She was . . . ' – *chop-chop-chop* went the knife, slower and slower – 'she made everything fun and exciting—'

'She's like that now.'

'—and she made me feel just right. I don't know how she did it.'

'Me too. She –' Eliza faltered and then started again. 'Dad said she was annoying. He said she was a show-off.'

Tom did not seem to hear this. 'And when she played the piano it was like she'd tamed it – like it was her pet wild animal.'

Eliza remembered Eliot stroking the lid of her Bechstein. She felt love for Eliot expand in her heart like a blown-up balloon. 'Tom, what's going to happen?'

'I don't know.'

'No one will tell me.'

'No one knows, not even your mum or dad.'

'But it's not fair.'

'No, I know. It's not.' This was what Eliot had said, and it was simple.

'People don't stay together. Not you and Kathy and not Gravel and Grumpeter either.'

'They want to, but sometimes they can't.'

'What about you and Eliot?' It just came out; she couldn't help it.

'We never were together,' said Tom. He did not ask her what she meant and nor did she ask him anything else because just then his telephone bleeped in his pocket. It was a message from Martha: *Got too late will come in the morning all love.*

Eliza put the sausage-pricking fork down and went back to her bedroom, climbing the stairs on all fours as she used to do when she was a much smaller child.

There was a hole in this holiday and Clive knew he was the one slipping through it. He did not belong with the other four in their warm, gathered pocket; he was the toy that would be dropped on the road and not missed.

He was distanced from Eliza, and Tom – although he had not mentioned that long-ago incident – spoke to his brother with the politeness of a stranger.

My house, my daughter, Clive told himself, but these were just

179

title deeds: Tom had taken possession with his great, open heart, and there was no competing with that.

Clive knew that Stan and Jack had wanted to come to the shop because, for them, a trip in the Space Wagon meant an adventure, but he could not stump up the energy for a song or a guessing game. They were quiet in the back seat and it dawned on Clive, to his shame, that they were frightened of him.

In the shop Stan cheered up and stuck his head in the freezer. 'Ice-cream!' he shouted, and Clive got out a tub.

Jack ran a hand along the chocolate bars in an experimental fashion, looking over his shoulder to see if Clive would take the hint. Longing to make friends, Clive said, 'You can choose one for each of us,' but in the end Jack took so long that Clive picked up a box of Maltesers and told Jack to put the others back.

'No,' said Jack. Clive, exasperated, had to uncurl one of his tiny, gripping fists from around a Kit Kat, and the other from a Milky Way. Jack began to cry, scattering his treasures.

Stan told him to shut up and the man behind the till peered over the counter in dismay. Clive exclaimed, 'Stop it, both of you!' The rest of the mission was accomplished in silence.

Clive felt as unfamiliar and lost as if he had been placed with a foreign family, in a different country, to learn a new language. Back in the car he rattled the gearstick and stared down at it, wondering where he would find 'R' for reverse. On the way home he overshot the turning to his – Martha's – her father's – wretched house and had to drive on for a half mile before he could turn round. He swore, without thinking, and arrived back in the yard to the tune of 'Bloody! Bloody! Bloody!' from the back seat.

'Fun trip?' laughed Tom, coming to the door with a tea towel slung over his shoulder.

In the morning everyone was gluey-eyed and cloth-headed, more tired and cross even than on school mornings. Tom had barely slept in his tent and Clive had been sleepless on the sofa.

'Holidays,' said Tom, shaking his head and pouring coffee, 'are knackering. Hospital hours are so much more relaxing.'

After munching, gulping, stretching and roaring he said, 'What we need is a walk,' and the children pulled on their boots.

It seemed to Clive as if Tom could conjure a landscape out of the air for the exclusive adventures of his faithful, merry band. They crossed fields, leaped over streams and rummaged in woods Clive had not known about and never visited – but then, to his surprise, their path led them alongside a river that he recognised. He had been here once before, long ago.

When he realised that this was the place where he had seen the otter, he felt apprehension beat a pair of dusty wings inside him. A gusting summer wind blew into the trees that lined the river, turning them white as they lifted their leaves to the sky.

'How did you know about this place?'

'I looked at one of Martha's maps.'

Martha. Clive cringed when he heard her name. He dreaded returning to the house, where she would be waiting.

'I've been here,' Eliza said, 'with Mum.' She took Tom's hand and swung from it. 'We had a picnic, when I was little. You were working,' she turned to accuse her father.

'I've been here too,' said Clive. 'Once, before you were born.'

Jack began, 'Dad—'

But he was interrupted by Stan, 'Dad—'

'Wait, Stan, I was—'

'Shut *up*. Dad—'

Tom said, 'Jack first, please,' and Stan dropped behind, whacking bits of bracken with a stick.

'I can't remember now,' admitted Jack.

Tom laughed. 'Pff! You are a pair of clots!'

Eliza made a game of walking with Tom. She tried to match her stride to his and had to skip to keep up. 'It's like we're in a three-legged race,' she said, breathless and laughing.

Clive's nerves hummed like wires in the wind.

He had asked Tom, 'Did Martha get the job?'

'I don't know. They kept her late, that's all I know.'

'Is that good?'

'Depends who's asking,' Tom had said, flinging spoons into the dishwasher. 'What's good for her is probably bad for you. Have you thought about Eliza moving to France?'

No.

Beside the river, a plan took shape in Clive's mind: escape. A road trip. A visit to his father. Stopping off at châteaux and vineyards on the way. A dust-stained arrival. His father's welcome: a honey-coloured terrace; a canopy of vines; a bottle of rosé waiting, cold and fragrant. 'I might go and visit Dad,' he said aloud, speaking over the chucking jackdaw voices of the two boys.

Eliza shot him a look, and Tom said, 'Bit of an odd time to go on holiday, isn't it? Might be better to wait and see—' He was interrupted:

'There's a rope!'

'Across the river!'

Tom looked and said, 'So there is.' With the children hung around him like three little pilotfish he trotted ahead to a place where, knotted between two trees, a rope had been slung across the open water.

Clive stepped up behind the others, cautious. He saw the careless swing of the rope in the wind and read in it the grin – the challenge – of a malevolent spirit. Here the river ran deep, rolling a path downstream with lazy menace. Its puckered surface stirred as if knots of eels were rummaging through its depths. The water reflected the dull, mutinous gaze of a clouded sky. Clive felt a premonition and was hot and cold at once, as if he had a fever.

'Who's it for?' Eliza asked.

'Anyone who can reach it,' said Tom. The boys jumped as high as they could, and Eliza got on to her tiptoes, but the rope was still beyond their fingertips. 'See?' Tom said. 'Grown-ups only.'

Jack said, 'Can you, Dad?' Tom stretched up a hand and pulled the rope into his fist.

'Can you go across?' asked Stan, more curious than challenging.

183

At once, Jack was distressed: 'No! Don't. I don't want you to.'

'Nor do I,' begged Eliza. 'Please don't.'

Tom said, 'All right, I won't.' He let go, and the rope swung free.

It crossed, Clive estimated, thirty feet of water. It was no distance at all – just a few strides. He heard a voice scoff, 'But it's nothing!' Too late he caught his tongue – he had spoken without thinking.

They all turned to him. Tom said, 'Well. Hear that, Eliza? Your dad says it's easy.'

'Not *easy*,' Clive stammered. 'I said it's not far, that's all.'

'I'll go first, shall I, Clive?' Tom was mocking him. 'While you limber up?'

Eliza stepped back from them all and stood one leg. Her teeth chattered. 'Please,' she begged, wringing her hands, 'don't.'

'Don't worry,' Tom said. 'I'm closely related to a chimpanzee – didn't you know? – so I'm good at this sort of thing.' He took off his sweater, held it out for Eliza to hold, and began to do a comic routine of stretches and leaps as if he were warming up for a session of gymnastics. 'Just oiling the wheels,' he said, jogging on the spot and swinging his arms.

Eliza, despite her fears, began to giggle and hid her face in his jumper.

Clive felt the prickle of poisonous envy. 'You're not really going to, are you?' His voice thickened and tightened as he spoke.

'But it's nothing!' Tom mimicked Clive. 'There's nothing to it!' He dusted his palms and caught the rope above his head in both hands. Then he pulled up his feet and secured them, crossed over one another, so that he was hanging like a three-toed sloth. He grunted – '*Ouf* – *Prrff* – *Whuf*' – under his breath as he adjusted himself into the right position, and then he said in a decided voice, 'Right.' With even, regular movements he shunted away from them, along the rope and across the river: *shift arm – drag feet – shift arm – drag feet.*

Jack's mouth fell open.

Eliza said, 'Wow.'

'I bet I could do it!' This was Stan. 'Dad, let me!'

In no time at all Tom had landed on his feet on the grass of the opposite bank. His three admirers cheered him and he took a little bow. Then he lay down flat on his back and from this position he called to them, 'That was harder than it looked.'

'It looked hard!' said Eliza. 'Really hard!' Her colour had returned and her voice was overjoyed.

'Now you've got to come back,' crowed Clive.

'Shall I wait for you?' teased Tom.

'No, Dad,' Eliza forbade him. 'You are *not* going to.'

On the opposite bank Tom got to his feet and clapped his hands. 'OK, here I come.' He slung himself under the rope and came shimmying towards them, head first and feet shifting up behind, inch by inch. Halfway back he stopped, hanging above the water. 'I'm *very* tired,' he teased, 'and I'm *very* hot . . . What about a dip?'

'No!'

'No!'

'No!'

Tom laughed, 'Fooled you!', and continued to wriggle in

their direction. When he was within reach of the grass he dropped at their feet with a thud and spread himself out on his back.

The three children knelt beside him and Eliza – whose face had flowered with relief – fanned him with a scrap of bracken. 'Are you all right?' she whispered. 'Tom?'

Tom's T-shirt had turned from grey to black with sweat. He lay with his eyes closed and said, 'Not . . . quite . . . ready to get up . . .'

'Dad that was so cool –' Jack was awestruck.

'You must be really strong –' Stan jumped up and leaped on top of Jack to wrestle him to the ground – 'like me!'

Eliza stayed beside Tom. 'I should put one of those tin foil things on you,' she said, 'like after the marathon.'

It was this voice – worshipping – that made Clive say, 'OK: my turn.'

Eliza looked up at him from her kneeling position and said, 'Dad, no *way*.'

Tom sat up. 'Seriously, bro,' he said, 'it's knackering. Forget it.'

'I don't want you to,' Eliza said. 'Don't.' She got to her feet.

But Clive had taken off his jacket. 'Back in a minute,' he said to Eliza. He reached up to take the rope between both hands. 'Worried I might do it, are you, Tom?'

'No, I'm worried you might not.'

'We'll see,' said Clive, and swung himself into position as Tom had done. The four spectators fell silent.

Clive, to his surprise, felt quite comfortable and secure. The bristling stoutness of the rope was reassuring, as if it were alive and on his side – as if he had taken hold of an obliging carthorse by the tail. Now he began to move.

Although it might not have been the easy *one-slide-two-slide* of Tom's crossing, he was not ashamed of himself. He felt confident. In a few moments – he could somehow feel the difference in the empty air below his back – he had left the bank behind and swayed from side to side above the roiling surface of the river.

The knowledge that a fall, now, would end in a cold soak had a curious effect: Clive's nerve stalled and his strength began a rapid ebb as if a plug had been pulled from a basin. He frowned at his two fists, clenched in front of his eyes, and at the empty grey sky behind them. Each motion took more effort than the one before it, and each had to be followed by a pause. *Drag; cling.* Begin again. *Drag; cling.* He shifted forward inch by inch.

He was surprised by how soon and fast the pain came, and also by how difficult it was to breathe. His lungs were pincered by his ribs and his chest was squeezing his poor, struggling heart. His brain shouted only one message, over and over, to his arms and legs: *Come down from there!* A different command – *Keep going!* – seemed absurd; unsound; insane. Co-ordinated movement was beyond his strength and somehow his intellect. Pain made concentration impossible. His initial rhythmic motion was replaced by grabbing, jerking and shunting at random. A colossal weight seemed to hang from his waist, pulling him down, and a hot, metal rod seemed to press at his shoulders. The rope – his friend a moment before – now sawed itself a gutter in his palms.

Tom called, 'You're doing really well,' from the bank.

Clive set his jaw. *You think I will fall but I won't.*

'Hang on, Dad.' Tears blotted Eliza's voice.

Tom said, 'If you do fall, try to go in feet first. Don't splat on to your back, it'll bloody well hurt.'

'You said "bloody"!'

'Shut *up*, Stan!' Eliza rounded on him.

I will not fall.

With every forward inch Clive felt the swell of rage inside, but he could not remember where it had come from or for whom it was meant. Eliot? Martha? Tom? He ground his teeth – this anger was distracting him – slowing him – pulling him down –

I can do this.

He remembered that people who completed incredible feats of human endurance often said afterwards, 'I wanted to give up, but a little voice inside my head told me to keep going, and then I found that I could.'

With a determined inner voice, Clive spoke to himself: *Go on. You can. You must.*

But within another second – and to his great surprise – his strength gave out and he fell.

Arriving at the cottage Martha made a cautious entrance and went about with quiet steps as if someone – an invalid, perhaps – were sleeping upstairs. A squad of empty mugs hunkered in the sink and the milk had been left on the counter but the house seemed replete, as if it had swallowed its guests.

She pushed open the door to Eliza's bedroom with one finger but did not go in. From the landing she looked down at two tents, shivering on the grass. The wind was getting up. In the sitting room she saw the discarded blanket and guessed that Clive had slept there. *Clive.* She turned from the room.

This was her domain and she felt confident of it, but still she did not know quite what to do with the day. Where were the others? She had imagined them all coming out of the house to greet her, and Eliza running into her arms and asking, 'Did you get the job?'

Yes!

But there was no one here to tell. Finding a corner of cheese in the fridge she smeared it with Branston's from the jar and nibbled at it, staring through the kitchen window at the trembling holly. Beyond it the grass in the hayfield rippled to silver and back again. After the cheese she ate a Malteser which had somehow rolled into the cutlery drawer. Still her mood refused to settle. It was the wind, making her restless.

She pictured herself and Eliza, bobbing on uncharted waters in a little boat. *Do I dare begin another life?* She thought of Clive and of what he would say. Worry shadowed her face.

Abandoning the kitchen Martha went into the sitting room and, despite a guilty feeling as she did it, lay down on the sofa where Clive had slept. She pulled his blanket over herself and pressed a cushion under her cheek.

She hoped no one would come in and catch her. What was wrong with her today? She did not have the nerve for confrontation; she did not have the strength to stand tall against this gusting wind. She only wanted to lie here in the quiet and stare through the glass at the galloping sky.

*

The first thing Clive saw when he burst his head out of the water was Eliza's face, staring at him with her eyes and mouth wide open. Tom was scrambling down the steep bank towards him and being torn at by brambles. At the water's edge he shouted, 'Are you OK? Can you swim all right? Kick off your shoes.'

But Clive could not reply – he had concerns beyond his footwear. The water was pulling his clothes in all directions and he could not touch the riverbed with his toes. This was unexpected. He looked at the bank and saw that Tom had moved – no, that he, Clive, had moved; the river had moved him – and Tom was having to keep pace.

'Dad,' cried Eliza – really cried – from the grass.

Clive opened his mouth to say, 'I'm fine,' but his head and shoulders went under and now his arms fluttered above his head and stayed there, tangled in his shirt which seemed determined to come off. Arms up and feet down Clive sank, like a dart, until his toes touched the bottom. He pushed off with all his strength but to his surprise the mighty kick he had intended was only a feeble shove which did not deliver him to the surface. *Again!* he told himself, *kick again!* But his legs hung like ribbons and refused.

He was startled – *Oh! Is this how it will be?* – and opened his eyes. With a wide gaze he looked at the water that heaved and coursed around him. His mouth gaped. Exhaustion thumped him like a thrown brick. He spun – limp and useless – in the water.

And then a sharp and terrible pain as his hair, ear and head were clutched and yanked by pinching fingers – *Tom!* He was let go again – grabbed again – plucked – pulled – dropped. A fist plunged into his armpit and now he was hoisted and flung out of the deep water and into the shallows. He skidded on to the muddy shore, turned to a paste where cows had stood to drink. With a splash and a thud Tom, soaking wet, fell down beside him.

'Christ,' said Tom, 'my shoulder –' He turned from hands and knees on to his back, clutching one arm. 'You *idiot* . . .'

But Clive could take in nothing but the racing sky above him; he could not move one single muscle in his body.

'You idiot,' said Martha to Clive. Hearing the approach of shrill, competing voices she had come to the door of the cottage and stood with folded arms and flashing eyes like the vengeful Boudicca.

'River –'

'Shoes got swished away –'

'Glug glug glug –'

Eliza, silent and pitch-faced, pushed past her mother.

'Where are you going?'

'To my room.'

Tom was white with pain. 'Your bloody husband.'

'*Your* bloody brother,' Martha retorted. She was furious: there would be no moment now to boast about her job and she felt the air escaping from her triumph like a punctured balloon. Clive's failure had shot down her success.

The culprit himself said nothing, limping past all of them and locking himself in the bathroom.

*

Clive stayed upstairs, much to Martha's annoyance, and she was forced to take her mood out on the pots and pans. She made spaghetti with tomato sauce and complained to Tom who lay on the sofa and unbuttoned a packet of Nurofen Plus.

'Have I come all this way to do the cooking and cleaning? What a surprise.' She heaved a boiling mountain of pasta into a colander. 'After tea I'm going to the pub. I want to have some fun.'

'Good idea,' said Tom in a faint voice.

Now Martha was cross with him. 'And yes I got the job, thanks for asking.' She took another swig of wine.

Cycling to the pub she began to feel better inside (wine) and out (lipstick). She felt the wind behind her and fury blow out of her hair as she sailed along.

Eliza had been sulky. 'The pub? But you've only just got here!'

No one had wanted to eat their supper, which made Martha crosser still. 'What's wrong with it?'

'Black bits,' Jack had explained when Stan pushed his bowl away. 'Ours doesn't normally have them.'

Martha had aimed a furious look at Tom, but he was still on the sofa and dozy with painkillers.

As she approached the pub Martha saw that there was something going on. She put on her front and back brakes to slow down and give herself time to look.

A large, round tent with its sides pinned up stood in the

field, and cars were parked all over the grass. A blackboard leaned against a post by the gate: 'The MacCoustics! Tonite! Dancing!' Martha skewed to a standstill, putting out her feet and yet almost tipping over. Was she drunk? She thought back over the day and made a rough calculation: piece of cheese plus Malteser plus two glasses of wine equals drunk. The front wheel wobbled in confirmation.

What the hell: she had wanted to have fun and now she would. She pictured breakfast in the morning and herself saying, *It was such a laugh, you should have come!* to Tom and Clive. She was here now, she was wearing lipstick and she had twenty quid in her pocket. She would smoke cigarettes, drink cider and dance.

She tied up her bike to a post and approached the gate where a girl – dressed in tiny black shorts and a striped bikini top – stepped forward to take her money.

'Just the one?' she asked Martha. 'It's six quid for one and ten for two.'

'Oh,' said Martha, 'there's only me, I'm afraid.' She handed over a ten-pound note.

The girl seemed to smirk, shrug and tug up the strap of her bikini in one sardonic movement. She handed Martha change, saying, 'Have fun.'

Martha flushed. She mumbled a reply and turned towards the tent, clutching her coins and feeling exposed for the sham that she was: not a tiger like Eliot but a mothy old lioness, lost without her family group. The wine jumbled the thoughts in her head and she rattled the coins in her hand, suddenly close to tears.

But here was the tent and there was the bar and she must be brave – she must be – for this was her new life: separated and alone. These pods of friends who were standing, chatting and laughing a private hubbub – they could all be new friends of hers, if she chose.

Inside the tent were bales of straw, a makeshift bar and a stage. Lots of people – cider-warmed – were clustered on the grass. Some were older – affable, grey-haired men in waistcoats and rolled-up sleeves – and some were young and glowing, laughing in ripples. Children, big and small, threaded in and out to chuck fistfuls of straw at each other, pouncing with sudden shrieks and giggles. Looking at them Martha felt a three-note chord plucked in her heart: pleasure; sadness; longing. She felt her aloneness like a missed step.

A drink: that was what she needed. She went to the bar, bought half a pint of cider in a plastic cup, drank it in slow sips and looked around her. She watched the children playing, thought of Eliza and felt a plunge – two missed steps – of guilt. *Eliza.* She had left her behind when she could – should – have brought her.

Martha swallowed the thought in a gulp and turned back to the barman.

Apart from a ringing, stinging pain in every fibre of his being, Clive was unharmed. From an upstairs window he watched Martha pedal away down the track. When she had wobbled out of sight he got up, staggered downstairs, ate a plate of spaghetti and drank three cups of tea. Then he went to watch television with the others.

After the television had been switched off and Tom had taken the twins outside to persuade them into their sleeping bags, Clive went to Eliza's room. She was lying under her duvet with her biggest muffling headphones set over her ears. When Clive sat down beside her feet she did not move but watched him with huge eyes. She was trembling like a trapped mouse.

'What are you listening to?' he asked.

'Piano.'

'Will you turn it off?'

'No.'

He did not challenge her but waited a moment and then said, 'Are you all right?'

'Yes.'

Clive took a deep breath. 'I'm sorry, Eliza.'

Nothing.

'I am.' He felt very small and feeble; too weak to say much else.

Eliza moved one muffler from one ear. 'I asked you not to.' Her voice was cold and liquid as the river.

'I know.'

'I asked you not to,' she repeated. 'We all knew you couldn't do it; you were the only person who thought you could. I thought you were going to die.' She might have been an old lady speaking.

'It wasn't far to fall; it wasn't deep; I wasn't going to die.'

'I thought you were,' she said again. After another silence she said, 'Why don't you know what you can and can't do? Everyone else does.'

She did not say another word but put the muffler back on

her ear and shut her eyes. Tears pushed out from under her lashes and ran into the hair at her temples. Clive was too ashamed to stay and watch them. He got up and left the room.

Alone with Tom in the kitchen he got drunk and after that, maudlin and self-pitying. 'I let Eliza down,' he said, his head heavy with sorrow, wine and water. 'I let everyone down.'

'Not me,' said Tom, shaking his head in sober denial. 'I had absolutely no expectations of you in the first place.'

Cider really was delicious, Martha thought, smacking her lips. She noticed a warm, melting sort of drunkenness but it did not feel at all serious – it was only apples, after all. She smiled into her plastic cup.

In the tent the band materialised one by one and, crab-like, snuck up on to the stage. *We might play; we might not,* they seemed to say.

Martha perked up. This was pleasant. No one knew her. She could do as she chose. It was exciting. There were girls whose long hair lay placid on their bare, brown shoulders and men who rocked on their heels and laughed in unison. Screaming children pelted through the throng like a gang of swifts. They – these rowdy, rackety kids – had found a flag and come up with a game: whoever held it had to be chased and caught. The little children and the yelling dogs leaped in the air to try and snatch it.

It was the kind of game that would have caused Eliza's teeth to chatter in her head. 'Don't make me join in, Mum, please,' she would have begged, twining her fingers through her mother's. 'Can't I stay here with you?'

It was getting busy at the bar and Martha begged a cigarette from a boy who came to wait beside her. He had a nest of blond hair tied up in an orange bandana. 'Do you mind a rollie?' he asked in reply.

'No – but will you make it for me?'

'Honestly!' the boy joked, rolling his eyes. 'Here, take this.'

Martha held his glass while his nimble fingers rolled a cigarette. Now her hands were full and so he put it in her mouth and lit it before taking back his drink. Up close – his tanned hands sheltering the lit match – she saw he was not a boy, but only dressed like one. He might have been Tom's age, or Eliot's. 'Are you on your own?' he asked.

Martha gulped. 'Yes – well – I'm staying with ... someone, but she's ill.' When she said this Martha wondered whether every word she spoke tonight would be a lie. *No, I'm not married* – perhaps those words would come lolling out next. It was cider and loneliness, loosening her tongue, and she did not care; she only wanted to make a friend.

'I'm Jimmy.'

'I'm Martha.'

The band struck a chord and all the dogs barked; the crowd laughed, cheered and pressed into the tent.

The music began and Martha stared at the stage, holding her plastic cup of cider and her cigarette. She felt quite different. Sociable. If Clive were here she would have tugged him to the dance floor by his thumbs, laughing and saying, 'You know you'll like it once you're up there.'

Clive.

Now that she was drunk she considered him with a little more kindliness. If only she could stay drunk, she thought with a blurry grin, perhaps she could stay married. She was used to it, that was the trouble, but familiarity and easiness – neither of those had much to do with love. *Oh!* Her head ached with the beating pulse of these thoughts and the noise and clamour around her. *Stop my mind; stop my minding.* She was bored of herself. *I want to get out of my head.* 'Let's dance,' she said to Jimmy.

He hid their drinks at the bottom of a tent pole, the two cups tilted against each other. 'We'll come back for them,' he said. He led her towards the stage and they danced amid the merry wriggle, leap and clap of people round them. *This is fun,* Martha thought, and all at once she was loving it – music, dancing and Jimmy too who was sweet and did not stray too far but took hold of her hand every now and again, to turn her under his arm or spin a slow and solemn circle under hers.

As the music played and they plaited and wove, Martha could not decide whether she was sadder than she had ever been before, or whether this was the happiest moment of her life. All at once she felt sick. She stopped dead and rocked on her feet.

'Are you all right?' shouted Jimmy to her.

'Air –' she managed to say, 'sick –'

They stumbled out of the tent together, Jimmy laughing at her white face, and strolled across the field and up the slope, away from the tent and the cars. '*Ouff*,' said Martha. 'Too much cider; too much spinning; not enough to eat; cigarettes.'

'It was pretty hot in there,' said Jimmy. Then he took her hand and held it. She felt his fingers press her wedding ring and he asked, 'Does this mean you're married?'

'Yes,' she said. She waited for her head to stop whirling and then she added, 'Well, yes and no. I'm separated.'

She had not said this before: *separated. I am separated.* It didn't make sense. *We are separated* – that was better. But then: 'we'. She frowned; 'we' was not right. Could she ever be one person again? Eliot was always only one – 'She's a tiger – she goes around on her own' – but Martha belonged to other people – 'You're a lion, Mum. You have to be, because of me and Dad.'

Martha was separated; Eliot was unattached. 'She doesn't speak to her parents,' Eliza had said. 'She doesn't like them.'

Jimmy interrupted her jumbling thoughts and linked her fingers with his. Their two palms pressed together. *Am I doing that?* she wondered. Aloud, she repeated – as if perhaps she might convince herself – 'I'm separated.'

'Good,' said Jimmy in reply. With a deft movement he swung her to face him – as if they were still on the dance floor – and then kissed her, pressing smiling lips against her startled mouth.

'Oh!' She made a surprised sound but of course she had known a kiss was coming since the first cigarette – she had as good as asked him for it: *Will you make it for me?* That was the way it worked. It was gratifying to have requested something in an old code – only an hour or so ago – and now to have received it. Success! At last there was something to show for this wretched day. She was buoyant with triumph; if Jimmy had not been holding her she might have bobbed away.

The kissing began again and now she was distracted and absorbed because it felt so good and she wanted more, she wanted to be overwhelmed and to stop the grind of that turning millstone in her head. She pushed and pulled at Jimmy a little bit, her hands on his collar; he in answer shifted so that he held her not by the hand but by the body – at her waist – at her shoulders – under her hair. His thumb touched her jaw and he fluttered light, guessing fingers on her cheek. She felt her legs begin to tremble.

She had not expected to want to do this quite so much. Desire made her stutter on her feet and open her eyes to watch Jimmy's dreamful face as he kissed her with lowered lashes and a little concentrating frown between his eyebrows.

This kissing might have been her idea but now she felt herself pliable, surrendering, delighted and longing in his hands, every touch of his lips leaving her more helpless. 'You're –' she began. *You're making me forget myself.* She was beginning to lose her bearings. *Wait; you're confusing me.* She had forgotten to breathe and now she could not; his mouth was over hers. Cider; cigarettes; the press of his lips and now of her own, kissing him back. Her head whirled: she had to decide what would happen next. *What was it*, she wondered, *that I wanted to do? Have I done it already? Shall I stop?*

Jimmy turned her hips towards him and pressed her with his

own. Martha felt her body turn liquid and hopeless. In a moment it would be too late to take a decision. 'You're so gorgeous . . .' he said, kissing her on her mouth and now away and down her throat – it made her blink and tip her head back with a pure, keen pleasure like spring warmth – and he murmured, 'What kind of man would let you go?'

The word – words – made Martha jump as if Clive had appeared next to them and touched her with a live wire. *What are you doing?* 'Oh!' she said, stepping back. 'Oh, no! I'm – What am I doing?' She put both hands up to her temples and gave a small, embarrassed laugh.

'What's happened?' asked Jimmy. His hands dropped to his sides. 'Are you OK?'

'Yes. No. I mean, sorry,' Martha said. She put her palms flat against his shoulders and took a deep breath, as sober as if someone had switched on a light. 'I'm so sorry; this is all wrong – I'm married, I have a husband . . .'

'I thought – you said – you were separated?'

'We are, sort of, I mean . . . oh dear, I've made a muddle. I'm sorry,' she said, 'I hate women who behave like this.' She frowned, standing in the half-dark, her head tilted to try and read his expression.

'Hey, don't worry,' said Jimmy. 'It's not a big deal; don't panic.'

Martha smiled, *phew*, and pushed her hair back off her face with both hands. She straightened her dress. She was ashamed of herself. 'I like you, and everything, but—'

'Look, it's only a bit of kissing; you won't go to hell.'

'No,' she said, shaking her head. 'I mustn't. I want to, but it's not fair.'

'OK,' he said. 'If you say so.' He slung an arm around her shoulders to steer her back down the grassy slope, towards the pub and the tent. 'C'mon then, naughty married lady,' he said.

Martha blushed. 'I'm sorry,' she said. 'It's not you—'

Jimmy laughed. 'No, I didn't think it was me,' he said, and kissed the side of her head.

Martha squeezed his hand, smiling in relief. He was just a kid! For him kisses came and went and did not matter.

'I wanted to, but then—'

'Look, it's OK, I swear. We're all allowed to change our minds, even about being married.'

Now she knew it really was all right and so she laughed. *It's nothing*, she thought.

Loosely clung together, they strolled down the hill. Martha's hair had escaped its ties and Jimmy walked with his warm hand placed underneath it, resting on the nape of her neck. She hung an arm around his waist and felt the muscles move under his shirt. She longed for him now even more than she had, but this was the way it would stay. She shook her head at herself.

It was getting dark and although the tent was lit – bright, noisy and crowded – the field was not. Cars were coming and going, lurching over the bumps in the grass and turning to park where their headlights found room. Everyone was occupied by the thump and tumble of the band. The children had taken no notice of the creeping dusk and were still playing their running, shouting game. They must be tired, Martha thought, as they hurtled past her. Those at the back were so little that she longed to clap her hands and call out, 'Time for bed!'. One small, tired boy trotted and walked on his own, breathless and pleading, 'Wait! Wait!'

Emotion flooded Martha, and almost made her stumble. *Eliza*, she thought. Her mind was filled with nothing – no one – else.

She remembered tears at night, and bleeding fingers in the morning. *Please, Mum, please don't make me go to school.*

'What is it that they do to you?' Martha had asked her daughter. 'If you tell me we can make them stop.'

But Eliza would not tell. 'No, Mum.' She shook her head. 'I can't.'

These children – flickering, glimmering, laughing as they ran in the dusk – would have frightened Eliza half to death and now Martha was frightened for her. *Eliza.* She wanted to go home.

'I ought to go,' she said.

'One more drink?' begged Jimmy, 'for the road?'

'You're lovely,' she said, 'but no.'

Jimmy hugged her goodbye and she felt the warm, strong weight of him, pressing her body. She put her cheek against his shoulder and closed her eyes. When he let go she felt weak.

Back at the gate she collected her bike and set off into the wind. The red light behind her saddle gave an occasional, feeble wink.

At the end of the lane she decided to walk, got off the bike and pushed it slowly up the track. Above her the sky glowed and flickered in black and white as the wind blew thickening strips of cloud past a confident, climbing moon. Martha looked up but the sight of it – a newsreel with an urgent message – made her so sad that she looked for the house instead, its sturdy shape at the top of the field with the black wood banked behind it.

There were no lights lit but she could make out the roof by the glint of its slates where the moonlight struck them. The walls beneath glowed a little luminous, as if daylight had somehow been trapped in the pores of the stone. Martha thought of the bats, huddled in the roof, and of Eliza in her bed under the eaves.

'What will happen?' Eliza had asked her, pleading.

'I don't know.' Martha had replied with a kind of defiance: *I don't know. Blame your father.* But blame was no comfort to Eliza; she only wanted to know where home was and whether she would be safe.

Tom's tents were still pegged to the grass but neither light nor movement came from inside. Martha trudged past, hoping that someone might hear her and welcome her home – 'Martha? Is that you?' – but no one stirred. In the yard she leaned her bike next to Eliza's against the wall and clicked open the kitchen door.

Once inside she felt weary and hungry but waiting for the kettle or even eating muesli out of the packet seemed too much of an effort. The lights in the room were dazzling; her eyes smarted and she wanted to be in bed.

At the sitting-room door she paused and listened. The up

and down sighs of Clive's sleeping breath came from the sofa. An idea took her by surprise: *I could curl up there beside him.* The sudden vivid longing shamed her like a blush. *His arms around me.*

She had to push the idea away – quick – step back – turn to the stairs – put a tethering hand on the banister and stand steady. *No.* She did not dare exhale. *What if he heard me? My breathing, or my beating heart?* She chided herself. *This moment of weakness will pass.*

She crept up the stairs – sober now, and sensible – and paused on the landing. Resting a hand on the wall, eyes shut, she wondered whether to go on up the stairs to Eliza's room. In that moment she smelled cider, Jimmy, tobacco and sweat on herself. She had better go to bed. Eliza would be distressed to see her like this, late and dishevelled.

In her own room Martha climbed on to the bed in her clothes, and lay down on her side. She pushed off her shoes, tucked her bare knees up into her dress and crossed her feet. Pulling a pillow under her cheek she blinked in relief. *Home.*

Then she fell asleep.

In the morning Clive's first thought was of Eliza. He remembered her words and the way she had said them: *Why don't you know what you can and can't do?*

He dragged himself off the sofa – *Oh God the pain that bloody rope* – and on to his feet. He would wake Eliza up and offer, 'Eggy bread?' It was her favourite; she must forgive him for that.

But the bed and the room were empty. She had gone.

12

The ringing alarm had sprung Eliza from her mattress like an electric shock. She had grabbed the clock and shoved it under the duvet, panicking and pressing every button she could feel with her fingers. At last the noise had stopped and her crashing heart had begun to decrease from *molto allegro* to *adagio*.

Wide awake and out of bed she had pulled back the curtain, peered out, and wondered, amazed, whether every day began like this. In her imagination, 'dawn' had always been a bright, yellow, rising sun and a burst of sunlight over the view, but here was something much more gentle and delighting. The familiar landscape outside her window looked as if careful hands had washed and dressed it, moments before her alarm. The grass had been sprinkled with glittering dew, and even the tents had been draped with jewelled cobwebs. There was no daffodil-yellow, beaming sun – not yet – but the polished, confident sky had seemed to promise its future attendance.

The sight had awakened Eliza's sense of purpose. She had pulled off her pyjamas and dressed in the clothes she had already laid out on the chair: socks, jeans, T-shirt, sweatshirt. She had made her bed look as lumpy as possible and read through her checklist: *Diary, rucksack, banana,* and then in bigger letters: *Money.*

Her mind had been filled with the journey ahead as she held her breath and skimmed downstairs like the family ghost, sneakers clutched in one hand and the other brushing the banister. On the landing she had crept around the edge to avoid the squeak and grimaced at her mother's bedroom door; downstairs she had tiptoed past the sitting room where her father had gone to bed.

In the kitchen she had drunk a glass of water and tied her ponytail, holding the elastic in her mouth while she smoothed her hair with both hands. She used to put her hair in two plaits for school when she was a little girl but then: 'Pig-pig-*pig*! Oink-oink-*oink*!' Etcetera. So it had become a ponytail.

'It's just nicer this way,' she had said to her mother. 'Mozart had a ponytail too.'

Everything on the list had been posted into her rucksack including all the twenty-pound notes she had found in her father's wallet and the credit card whose PIN number she knew. Eliza had felt bad about stealing but there was no other way – every time they took the train Martha said, 'It's so expensive!', so Eliza had known that her own £3.82 would not get her to London.

She had clicked open the kitchen door and slipped around it like a cat furring past a table leg. *Quiet-quiet.* But cold! It had made her gasp out and take a sharp breath in. *Quick-quick!* There was no time to faint or falter – she must leave right away before anyone woke. There was no moment to be frightened; none spare for second thoughts. She had grabbed her bike from the wall and snuck it away, silent and slow on the grass, until it was safe to jump aboard and pedal – *Go! Go!* – down the crunching gravel of the track.

Now on the train to London, tucked into a window seat with her headphones clamped on her ears, she felt not *vivace* or *tremolo* but *placido*. The hard part was over.

At break in the early days of school Eliza used to lock herself into one of the toilet cubicles with her feet tucked up on the seat so that no one could see her. Someone had written on the back of one of the doors –

Eliza Barkes
Eats Her Farts

– which was a good reminder of why she had to lock herself in. When the door to the corridor had banged open her heart had thudded in her chest so loud she had thought it would give her away. Sometimes she had forgotten to breathe when there were other people in there, and by the time the door slammed behind them she was nearly dead from not breathing.

It was bad enough if they came in to talk because talking could take ages, but the worst was if they came to talk about her. This had happened a few times and once she had not gone back into class after the bell but run out of the cubicle, out of the building, across the playground, out of the school and all the way home – not up to the front door but into the bin shelter where the snails lived and from where she could look up at the window of the flat.

Crouched by the stinking bins Eliza had peered through the glass at her mother. Martha had been sitting at her desk, typing, and then she had taken off her headphones to answer the telephone. It would be the school, Eliza guessed, ringing to say they had lost her. Now Martha was standing and had turned to face the window. Now a hand went up to her mouth and a frightened expression broke over her face as if the news had not been, 'Eliza's run away,' but, 'Eliza's dropped down dead'.

At that moment Eliza had felt so sorry for her mother that she had stepped out of her hiding place and into view. Martha, looking down on her, had placed a hand on the glass between them and spoken into the phone. Then she had hung up and come out of the front door with that expression still on her face like a stain.

Eliza had trembled up the front steps one by one with her own face washed with tears. When she reached her mother's legs she put her arms around them and held on.

Alone on the train to London, Eliza thought of her mother and how she had looked at that moment. She would look the same this morning, Eliza knew, when the empty bed was discovered. She felt a ripple of guilt which made her wobble, and then she shut the image from her mind. There were other things to worry about.

Being found out, for example. She planned to lock herself into the toilet if anyone looked at her or spoke to her in a suspicious way. This might include axe murderers, ticket collectors, the trolley woman, nosy old ladies or nasty children. It was a last resort (because the train toilet stunk even worse than the ones at her school) but it might be necessary and so she held it in reserve.

Getting out her diary she crossed out what she had achieved so far this morning:

Wake up!!
Money
Ticket
Train 0742

Still not crossed out was:

London 0954
Bus
Walk
Knock on door!!

She put the lid on her pen and looked out of the window, wondering whether this was the hardest thing she had ever done in her life. Hugging her rucksack to her chest she thought of other hard things, like learning to dive or the first rehearsal for *Oliver!* when she had thought she might be singled out or spoken to.

There was one thing which would always come top when it

came to 'Hardest Thing Ever': the playground. She had hated the playground more than anywhere else in the world – at the beginning she had dreaded it so much that she used to puke up her breakfast. Still she had gone there every day and crossed it alone like a limping wildebeest.

Today's trip she had done many times (with Mum or Dad or both) and it had always been easy and most often pleasant – it had never made her sick. The only different thing on this particular day was that she was alone, but Eliza did not feel more brave to be alone. In fact, she felt safer: she had experienced the treachery of friends and the brutality of strangers at school. Now she had discovered that parents could be treacherous and brutal too.

Taking the lid off her pen she wrote *Worst Things*, underlined it, and then thought about what to put.

When it had first started at school – the bad stuff – her mother had asked her, 'What are they doing to you? Tell me, please – then we can make it stop.'

Eliza had known this was not true and that there was nothing to be done. 'Don't tell' was the most important lesson she had learned at school. 'Nothing,' she had replied. 'There isn't anything.' Then she had buttoned her lip and picked at her fingers instead.

Now she was afraid again and although it was not of the playground it was the same fear: that what was bad today would be worse tomorrow.

She wrote down –

<u>Worst Things</u>
No more Eliot
No more piano

– and then stopped. There was something else, but she could not bring herself to write the word: *divorce*.

The idea of divorce had only occurred to her quite recently. When first her grandparents and then Tom and Kathy had split up, the separations had been couched in terms of geography: 'Grumpeter wants to live in France', and 'Tom's got a job in a different hospital'. Eliza saw now that while both those statements had been true they had only been partial truths. Peter and Tom had moved because their relationships had ended, not because they wanted to live somewhere new. Eliza had been deceived – how stupid she had been! Just a silly little girl, to believe what she was told. At that time her concerns had been as little as herself: would Gravel still have a Chocolate Orange? Would she still see Stan and Jack at Christmas? Now that she was older and knew more about people in general, and her parents in particular, she carried the word 'divorce' around with her like a furled umbrella on a cloudy day. *Just in case.* She did not want to be surprised by rain; she wanted to be prepared.

What would divorce mean for her? Two homes. Her heart pinned to each and stretched between them. Dad living somewhere else and maybe – if Mum got a real all-day job – a new flat for her too. That would mean another school and another *fucking* playground. The savage word roared in Eliza's head. She hated her parents. This was a rotten future in which nothing would be certain and all of her questions would be met with 'I don't know'.

It was when she thought of *no more home* that she felt as if she were the umbrella and that a gust of wind had blown her inside out to face a pelting rain. No one bothered to mend umbrellas – she had seen them dumped in rubbish bins on stormy days – because unless they stayed up they were useless.

Perched in the toilet cubicle on those dreaded, desperate days, Eliza had told herself that every second which passed, however bad it was, brought her nearer to going home. That was the way she had completed each day: one second after another, each one closer to the final bell. She had tucked her feet up on the plastic seat, bringing her knees to her chest, until she was curled like an anxious hedgehog or shut like a human clam. Nothing – no one – could prise her apart and get inside. Behind the locked door she had bent her head and pressed her closed eyes against her knees until her eyeballs hurt and she saw red and black in flashes. Behind the warm, rough smell of her skirt and her tights – *home* – she had smelled the sharp cut of disinfectant from the floor. That smell would make her tough, she had thought. If she breathed it in for long enough, it would harden her insides.

There had been no crying – not there, locked up safe with her feet off the floor – but only sitting, waiting, and dreaming of being at home.

Last night they had all – apart from her mother who had gone to get drunk in the pub – watched a programme on television

213

called *The Ultimate Fate of Our Universe*. Afterwards, Eliza had gone to her room and her father had come to talk to her. Once he had gone away again she got out of bed, opened the window and looked out.

It had been brought to her attention by the television programme that being a planet was a lonely business. Each was confined, by the laws of its own orbit, to a solitary life. They might all be called 'planet', but they were not related. There was no communication: if Saturn fell in the river and Jupiter went to the pub, Mars would have nothing to say on the matter at all.

Above the house a starlit sky had glittered behind scraps of blowing cloud. Eliza had leaned out of the window, trying to see as far as possible into the universe. She had squinted at the stars and into the spaces between them.

Then it had occurred to her that 'space' began right here, at her open window: there was nothing but a shred of cloud between the end of her nose and the edge of the universe. Her eyes had widened and all the breath had puffed out of her in surprise. *I'm spinning away.* She had become a spider turning slow, astonished circles down the drain; a sheet of paper drifting, helpless, into the yawn of the Underground tunnel. There was no 'up' or 'down' in space but only further and further away; she was tumbling, head over heels, into the limitless gap, and where she was going could not be called 'somewhere' or a 'place'. It was just a vacant, empty plot: *deep space*.

The ring of her cousins' voices had broken into her thoughts –

'Give me the torch!'

'No!'

'Give it!'

'No!'

– and Eliza had blinked: she was back on the earth, and back at the window. Garden, grass, tree and tent were all laid out below where she had left them. Torchlight had jumped and flickered through the walls of the tent and into the thick night air, sheltered to a soft and mellow stillness.

Those badgery boys knew nothing of these fears, and Eliza had wished she was ignorant too. Snuffling out there in the garden on the grass – with their torch and their funny rocking voices, question and answer like owls in the wood – they were not troubled by such terrors because they had each other. Eliza envied them. They spoke to one another as if one mind, shared between them, spoke with two companionable voices.

That was how she felt when she was with Eliot: as if they were side by side at the piano and playing with one hand each. Eliza would play the part of the right hand and Eliot the part of the left.

At that moment – leaning her cheek against the cool pane of glass, feeling the breath of the night and hearing her cousins speak in canon and fugue – two voices had seemed to strike up a dialogue in Eliza's own head. One had told her, *Go!* and the other, *But you can't*. Looking out of the bedroom window she had begun a spirited argument with herself that had ended when she crept into the kitchen and looked up the time of the morning train: *0742*.

*

What if home were no safer than the playground, or than outer space? Was this the very worst thing that could happen? The train pummelled on. Eliza held her pen over the page, not quite touching it. What if writing these words made them true?

All of a sudden she was tired – so tired she was not just drowsy but almost asleep and dreaming. She put the lid on her pen, leaned her rucksack on the window and let her head flop against it. Beyond the glass the blur of land and sky had grown pale: London. The cottage lay in country that was rumpled curves and burrows – a sleeping toy in an unmade bed – but London was edge and surface. Everything was exposed. Even leaves, blown into the playground from the street, were forced to dance in public circles by the wind.

Martha was white, sitting up on her bed in her clothes. *What? Gone? Where? Oh God –*

'Car keys,' Clive said, 'please, *now*. I'll go. You—'

'Go where?' She got off the bed and searched for the car keys in yesterday's jacket. 'Where has she gone? We're all here, for God's sake! Who would she –?'

She would not say the name – and nor would he – but they both knew where and who.

'Stay here,' he ruled, snatching the keys from her outstretched hand, 'and phone the stations. And the police. Find her bike. Get them to look on the CCTV. And phone my mother – I'll never beat the train – get her to go to Paddington and wait.'

'But—'

The door flew shut behind him, and she heard his feet go thumping down the stairs.

Tom telephoned Val who said, 'I'm not surprised, if you want to know the truth.'

'Save it, Mum,' said Tom. 'Just get to Paddington, will you?'

'She's a very angry little girl,' said Val. 'And with good reason.'

'Why are you telling me? I agree with you. Now can you get there?'

'Of course I can,' she said. 'There's plenty of time. Aren't I always telling you how close I am to central London?'

On the train Eliza was snapped awake by the sound of a voice that carried the flat, attention-calling resonance of a handclap.

'Right, everybody! Tickets, please!'

Eliza unzipped her rucksack and held hers in her fist, trying to even out her heartbeat by thinking of minims rather than quavers.

She could tell from the sound of the ticket inspector's voice that he was a man who loved his job. As he approached he spoke to each passenger: 'Hello there, thank you. Now, where are we off to? Lovely, thanks, there you are. Yes, madam, we are on time.'

Closer and closer he came. Why could she not have got one of those moody, silent ones? Today was a Sunday, and quiet. So far no one had said a word to her, and she had not needed to speak. She had operated two machines – one for cash and one for the ticket – but no living, breathing person had paid her any attention at all.

She knew the iPod would give her no cover and nor would it be any use to pretend to be asleep. The inspector would stand there – she had seen this happen to other people – repeating, 'Excuse me,' until she opened her eyes. Now he was here and it was her turn; she licked her lips like a bad dog.

'Hello, miss,' said the man. He looked at her, first over his spectacles and then through them.

Eliza made a bared-teeth smile and held out her ticket.

'Thanks very much.' The man held the orange rectangle in his hand and seemed to read every single word as if he had never seen one quite like this before. 'Where are we off to? London? On your own?'

Eliza did not trust herself to speak so she nodded.

'Aren't you grown-up.'

Was it a question? He seemed to expect a reply. Eliza cleared her throat and said, 'Yes I am.'

The man gave her back the ticket and she took one end, but to her terrible fright he kept hold of the other. Now she was stuck, frozen in place. 'Someone meeting you the other end, are they?' he said. His voice was kind but still it was the worst question in the world.

'Yes,' she gulped. 'My mum.'

'Very good, well done. I wish my little girl was as responsible as you are.' He let go.

For an awful moment Eliza thought she might start crying. Tears pricked her eyes and an enormous lump, as big as if she'd swallowed a whole loaf of bread, sat in her chest. She smiled – mainly to crinkle up her eyes and stop the tears popping out – and looked down at her rucksack. She took a lot of trouble over putting her ticket away and opening and closing all the zips.

The conductor looked at her for three-and-a-half more seconds – which she counted – and then turned to the next person and went on down the carriage: 'Hello, hello, here we are, tickets please . . .' Eliza thought that everyone must be looking at her. She stared out of the window until the red-hot feeling went away.

At last the train began to slow down and it passed an on-the-top Underground station. When she saw that round red-and-blue sign it was so familiar that Eliza felt as safe as if she really were being met off the train – as if Eliot had come from Hampstead in her little car to stand at the barrier and wave. Even though this was not the end of her journey Eliza felt like cheering and running up and down the aisle with her shirt over her head, like the boys did when they scored at football. Instead she joggled in her seat and grinned at her reflection in the windowpane. She made the face of a triumphant tiger at the swoop and dip of the neighbouring tracks which were slowing down and turning from a formless grey mash into a neat threaded pattern of ribbons and streamers.

Everything that had come out of her rucksack was zipped back into its pocket. She fished out her Oyster card and gripped it in her hand, so hard that its edges marked her palm. She struggled to contain her elation. She wanted to shout and boast to everyone on the train and to chant under her breath something that would accompany the clatter and swallow of the train's wheels over the points: *Eliot Fox, Eliot Fox, Eliot Fox.*

*

Eliot was not at the barrier but someone else, someone whom Eliza knew and loved, was there instead: her grandmother. Val was standing in a familiar pose – hands clasped in front of her and handbag tucked under one elbow – but she was looking older than usual. Eliza spent a moment staring – *Was it her? Could it be?* – before recognition spread like melted butter.

When she knew for sure that it was Val she wanted to laugh, cry and shout out her name. She slowed right down, faltering, and then speeded up and ran the rest of the way, saying, 'Gravel! Gravel!' under her breath.

Her grandmother caught sight of her and right away looked ten years younger, as if she had swallowed a miracle drink. She broke into a smile, stepped forward and met Eliza's running – *flying* – body with open arms. They both hung on.

'Oh!' Val exclaimed. 'Oh! Oh! Eliza!'

That was all she could say.

In a café at the station Val made telephone calls on the mobile telephone she kept for emergencies but did not know how to use. Eliza pressed the right buttons for her and then listened to one side of three separate but similar conversations with Tom, Clive and Martha. To each of them her grandmother said the same two sentences: 'Yes she's fine,' and, 'No, you can speak to her later.'

When the telephone was switched off Eliza stared into the swirled pink galaxy of her smoothie. She stirred it with her straw. She had not decided whether she was pleased or sorry to have been caught; she still wanted to see Eliot, but she loved her grandmother. Taking a deep breath she plunged her straw up and down and said, without looking up, 'I wasn't going to go home. I knew there was no one there. I was going to see my friend Eliot.'

'Eliot Fox?' asked Val, sipping her coffee and then putting the cup back in the saucer with both hands. She turned to Eliza with her expression interested and her head bobbed on to one side like a bird saying, 'Any more crumbs?'

'Yes,' said Eliza. She could not imagine there might be another Eliot in the world.

Now she looked up from the smoothie and through the glass in front of her at the station concourse. Hundreds of people streamed in different directions like a sudden flood of rushing water; rivers and rivulets made up of dark-dressed human bodies. The noise was tremendous and her head felt full of it. With longing – a longing that puzzled her – she remembered the peace and snug of the train carriage. Behind her the coffee machine clattered and gasped in sudden and violent eruptions and from overhead the tannoy droned instructions with polite but insistent menace. Eliza was anxious and overwhelmed; it was too much to bear. The station was enormous but she felt pressed on every side. No one seemed to be speaking but the noise of thousands of travelling humans was a deafening clamour. It felt dark and tight with bodies yet when she looked up there was nothing but air between her head and the station roof – a distant pattern of black and white – and beyond that the sky, which after all was outer space.

The ultimate fate of the universe felt near at hand. Here with her grandmother she might be safe but in the open air there was nothing to cling to. Eliza thought of what had happened yesterday – her father, the river and the circling, lonely planets – and what might come today. 'I don't want to go home,' she burst out. 'I hate it.'

Val did not seem perturbed to hear this news. She ate some cappuccino foam from her teaspoon. 'Tell me,' she said, 'how were you going to get to Eliot's house?'

Eliza swivelled her face up to look at her grandmother's. 'A bus?' she said. 'Or maybe two?' She did not mention the walking.

'Well,' said Val, 'why don't we do that? If you know where she lives. But we must send text messages to your parents, first, to tell them what we're up to.'

Then Eliza did start crying. She pushed the tall smoothie glass out of the way and bowed her head until her face rested on her fingers which she laid on the counter in front of her as if she were in church on Christmas Day. Val patted her between the shoulders and produced a tissue to soak up the tears. They remained in this pose for several minutes until they were interrupted by the café man who shouted, 'Cheese-and-ham toasted panini!' and plonked a plate down between them.

Both Val and Eliza laughed, and the spell was broken. When Eliza looked up, squeezing the damp tissue in her palm, the people in the station were not surging up to the glass in front of her like a dirty tide but had returned to the bustle and hurry of their individual journeys. The noise was not a fearsome crescendo that bullied her ears – it did not seem to be ungovernable or hectoring at all. Instead it was something more sociable and perhaps even well-tempered: the continuous, measured putter of different feet criss-crossing the smudged, white floor.

222

13

Val told Clive, 'She's fine,' and then, 'No, not while you're driving. You can speak to her later.' He did not argue; he felt relief surge from his body in a churning, white wave. Taking his foot off the accelerator he watched the needle drop below ninety. Eliza was safe and there was nothing to be gained by breaking the law. It occurred to him – with sudden urgency – that he would have to stop for a pee.

But a few minutes later his telephone delivered a message which drove all ideas of respite from his head: *We are going to see Eliot Fox.* Clive's foot went down on the pedal again and the sign for 'Motorway Services' – the coffee cup and the cosy-looking single bed – flashed into his rear-view mirror.

The sight of Eliza's empty bed had eviscerated Clive with the swift, efficient scoop of a mechanical claw. Now he pictured his innards in a dirty grey pile at the roadside, where the grit and rubbish was scattered and flung by the blast of traffic. That was where he belonged. He had put himself there: he felt the rummage of a rat, heard the scornful chuckle of a magpie and cringed at the blare and whisk of passing cars.

The cold of the river had stripped him; the empty bed had gutted him. Whatever skin and bone remained would be put in the stocks and made to face what he had cowered from all these years: the shaken fist, the chanted slogan – *What have you done? What have you done?* – and the punishment he deserved.

There had never been a reason, until today, for Clive to be afraid of his daughter. Now he was terrified: the threat of disappearance gave her absolute power. He would have confessed any crime, begged forgiveness of any person and accepted any sentence for the return of his daughter's affection.

On the night of her musical, saying goodbye, Eliza had put both arms around her father's neck and whispered into his ear, '*I* don't hate you, Dad. I love you.' She had clung like a kitten. But now? Did she love him at all? She had run to Eliot Fox; she had gone of her own accord. If she did not want to cling Clive could not make her.

His telephone rang. 'Eliot's taking us on to the Heath.' Val said it in the special, bright voice which she saved for momentous occasions: 'The Queen Mother's dead,' or, 'Your father's moving to France.' 'It's such a lovely day,' she went on, 'we might have a picnic.'

Picnicking weather had come and gone by the time Clive set foot on Parliament Hill. Up he toiled, one slow step after another, a dirty wind blowing at his back and the tarmac path beneath his feet glued with the fruits of a London Sunday: dog mess, chewing gum and spilled ice-cream. He stopped to look up at the reaching trees and the whipped, white sky.

He seemed to have become separated not just from his family but from ordinary human traffic, discourse and activity. People surrounded him, heading down the hill and home, and he scanned each summery face as it passed, searching for something familiar.

At every side were children, but they did not reassure him – they were nothing like Eliza. These tumbling, laughing creatures did not resemble her at all: last night she had spoken to him not with the voice of a child but with the sorrow and solemnity of a judge. He longed to hear her call out, 'Dad!', in the voice with which she had claimed him all her life, but he felt so lost, so bereft and so unlike himself that he wondered if he would be recognised.

Self-pity made Clive stumble; he felt the jostle and throb of his crimes. For a moment he faced the blue-shadowed city and heard its arterial rumble. Then he turned and pressed on his way, upwards and alone.

At the top of the hill that coursing bass note was overlaid with fluting treble sounds: the clatter of children's laughter, the yip of a running dog and the whir of a kite overhead. A huge box overflowed with rubbish and patient crows strode round it, stiff-legged on the grass.

'You'll see us,' Val had said with confidence. 'We'll be there.'

225

Clive turned this way and that, shading his eyes, staring at strangers and away again, pleading –

Oh, Eliza –

– And there she was, already on her feet and running towards him.

Clive, half-blinded by relief, stumbled to meet her and she threw herself into his arms, open and delighted. Then – within a second – she had gathered up her feelings and angled out of his embrace.

'Are you angry?' she asked.

He tried to hold on to her – those shoulder-blades like wings under his fingers, how he loved them! Those little elastic arms, that scented hair in its ponytail! If only she would cling to him, grip him as he did her! *Oh! Oh! Eliza! Please! –* but she slipped out of his grasp and to the ground.

For a moment he was so desperate he could not answer. 'No,' he said in the end, 'not angry. Scared. I was scared.'

He kissed his mother, and even squeezed her hand. 'Thanks, Mum.'

She said, 'Well,' and, 'Here we are,' but that was all. Her expression was inscrutable.

'Where's Eliot?' Clive looked around.

'She had to go,' Eliza said.

'You've only missed her by a minute,' Val said. She turned, looked and pointed, 'There!'

'Dad—'

'You two stay here – I want to talk to her.'

'Clive, are you sure—'

'Dad, don't be mean! It wasn't her fault!'

Clive set off at a run and shouted, 'Eliot!' but the figure kept on walking away, under the trees and out of sight. He followed – saw the flicker of her figure in the shade – called her name again, but she did not stop. It was only when he had run right up behind her and said, 'Eliot, please –' that she swung to face him.

'What do you want?'

Her question was so abrupt that Clive stepped back as if he had been shoved in the chest. *What did he want?* He took short breaths to calm his heartbeat, wondering what he would say. Into his focus swam something bright: a little gold bee, pinned to Eliot's collar.

'You found it,' he said.

Eliot lifted her thumb to the brooch and gave it a rub. 'It's not the same one.'

Clive quavered. Would Tom appear beside them, like a genie from a lamp? He was afraid. *What did he want?* He opened his mouth. 'I want to say sorry,' he said.

Eliot searched his face. 'For what?'

'For all of it.' Clive swallowed. 'For everything.'

'All of *what?*'

'For what happened on your birthday –'

'What did happen? Tell me.'

She waited, poised and expectant; Clive felt the breath of the sharpened steel.

He hesitated.

'You can't even say the words.' Her voice was scornful.

Now with the sudden complex sensation – a fullness; a prickling – that he might be about to weep or vomit, Clive

227

found his voice. 'What else do you want from me, Eliot? *I'm sorry.* Isn't that enough?'

Eliot did not reply but stood with folded arms. Clive could not hold her look. He raised his eyes to watch a canopy of bruised, dark leaves shift and move behind her, shaking a dappled shade on to her shirt and her fair head.

'You're sorry today,' she said, after examining him a moment. 'I believe that.' It seemed to be a concession.

Now Clive did look at her, wondering. *Will I ever be rid of her?* Insight crept along his veins, as cold as melting snow.

'You're sorry today,' she said again, 'because you're scared. You want to buy Eliza back, with "sorry".'

'No,' Clive faltered, 'no –' but he knew she was right.

'Not everything is fair, Clive,' Eliot went on. 'Some things are unfair, and there's nothing to be done about it.' She tilted her head and looked him over. 'Not even "sorry".'

'Please –' Clive flailed, 'please –'

She waited, cool and still, until he found the words and dragged them into the open:

'– leave my family alone!'

This was what he wanted: *Leave my family alone!* He wanted Eliot – all trace and memory of her – to vanish into the air from which she had sprung.

Eliot seemed to be prepared for this – she seemed to have expected nothing less. 'Now I believe you,' she told him.

In the silence which followed she shifted on her feet as if to leave – she even seemed to move a little away – but then she turned back, lifted her head and met his eye. 'But your family, Clive,' she said. 'What do you think *they* want?'

She waited for an answer, but Clive did not reply.

Now with a light, slight smile – just the curl of it at her mouth – Eliot walked away.

'Did you catch up with her?' Val asked.

Clive had returned to the place where she and Eliza sat. He stared at them both. He felt as if a hundred years had passed.

Eliza was distressed. 'It wasn't her fault, Dad,' she told him. 'She didn't know I was going to run away. Please don't be horrible to Eliot.'

'I wasn't,' Clive managed to say, and then, 'I won't be. I know it wasn't her fault.' He was close to tears but a nagging fear, tugging at his head like a bridle, kept them in check.

In the car on the way back to her house, Val sat in the back seat and went to sleep – or pretended to. She rolled up her jumper, very small and neat, and slid it under her head and over the strap of the seatbelt. 'Don't mind me,' she said. 'I might nod off. It's all the excitement.'

When her eyes had been closed for a few moments Clive began to speak to Eliza.

'Please promise me you'll never, ever, *ever* do that again. Promise.'

'I promise.'

'Swear.'

'I swear.'

'We can talk about everything, can't we? You don't have to run away?' He was pleading.

Eliza did not answer. Her elbow, resting on the window

frame, seemed to keep collapsing under her so that she slumped against the door. She must be very tired. 'What time did you get up?' Clive asked.

She had to clear her throat to speak. 'Early,' she said. Then she remembered, 'It was beautiful. It was –' But she stopped.

'What?' Clive wanted her to talk to him.

'Nothing.' The details of her adventure seemed to be private.

'Was it ... were you scared?'

'No. I wanted to go, and that stopped me being scared.'

Now Clive did not want to hear any more.

'The man on the train was nice,' she went on. 'The ticket man. He said I was grown-up.'

Clive did not respond. After a few minutes he said, 'You know you can't get me and Mum back together like this, don't you? It's not the right way.'

'I know.'

Clive had not expected this reply. He tested her again, saying, 'It has to be us who decides.'

'OK,' said Eliza, and yawned.

Clive was perplexed and alarmed. This resilient, mysterious person – who was she? He tugged at the string in his hands but the kite flew up regardless.

The rest of the journey to Amersham passed in silence, but for the *tock-tock-tock* of the indicator. There was one 'sorry' left in Clive's head, rolling around like the last Malteser, but he did not say it.

14

Awake at dawn, Martha watched the sky begin to blush as the day came. She thought of Eliza and wondered whether every sunrise, from today and for ever, would remind her of yesterday: the day her daughter had run away.

She pictured Eliza's journey and its obstacles: cycling to the train through the cool, white bloom; setting her small, stickered bike in the rack; withdrawing cash from one machine and tickets from another; shivering on the platform as she waited for her train. And all of this to get to Eliot Fox.

Martha had asked Eliza, last night on the telephone, 'What made you go? Was there one thing?' *Please don't say it was me.*

But Eliza had not wanted to confide. 'No. I just . . .' and then her voice had drifted away.

'There's nothing for you to worry about,' Martha had stated.

This blatant untruth had not been contradicted – there had been no response at all.

Martha had tried again. 'Don't worry about things that might not happen.'

Now the silence had spoken: *But that's what worry is.*

'Eliza?' Had she put down the telephone and walked away? 'I love you,' Martha had pleaded. 'Everything's going to be fine.'

Tom had left as soon as he knew that Eliza was safe. He had dismantled the tents, buckled his sons into the Space Wagon and driven away. 'Eliza would rather be with Eliot,' he had said, 'and so would I.'

Martha had stared at him, dumbstruck. After his car had pressed its way down the track she had gone outside and sat on the flattened grass where his tent had stood. *I'm sorry,* she had whispered, pressing the ground with her palms. *Please don't leave me.*

On the telephone to Clive, Martha had said, 'This has gone on long enough.'

No response – neither protest nor agreement – came in return.

'I will fix it,' she told him, 'if you won't.'

Lying on her side in the bed, Martha did not move. Outside the window the rakish green of the holly shook its leaves at a wide-eyed blue sky.

It had never seemed so quiet here. She had never felt as alone. This was what 'separated' meant: not kissing strangers, smart clothes and a new job, but alone and apart from the people she loved.

She wanted her family. She wanted her attachments to pull at her like kite-strings, keeping her both airborne and grounded.

Deep in her chest a dull pain ached like a bruise. *It's my heart,* she thought. She did not move – perhaps if she stayed quite still she could keep all hurt and all feeling in check.

Eliza ran away. If I had not gone to the pub and kissed Jimmy, Eliza might have stayed.

'It's only a bit of kissing,' Jimmy had said. 'You won't go to hell.'

The memory made her cringe in the sheets where she lay.

Incidents and accidents collided in Martha's head. She wanted to thread them into order like pearls on to a string, but they would only clash together and apart like marbles. There was no making sense of them.

There's been an accident.

Martha had said those words many times on that dreadful night.

After the ambulance, from the hospital, she tried to reach Clive again at his hotel. The same receptionist took her call but this time Martha gasped, 'There's been an accident. Please find him – you have to.'

Still there was no answer from Clive's room. 'His key is here,' the girl said, slick and efficient.

'There's a colleague –'

'Yes. Shall I try her room for you?'

'Yes – yes –'

'One moment.' There was no more 'please' or 'ma'am'.

Then an English accent: 'Belinda Easton speaking. Who is this?'

'It's Martha –' Martha wondered how her voice was stringing these words together when she did not seem to be giving it any instruction. '– Clive's wife. There's been an accident. A fall – stairs – head – hospital –'

It was not what Belinda said –

'All right. Martha? It's all right: I'll find him, I'll tell him and I'll get him on a plane.'

– but the tone of her voice, a mother's voice, that reassured Martha.

When Clive rang back she gabbled, 'I woke up and she was crying – Oh God oh God – They won't tell me anything – It was only for a second –'

Clive asked, 'What have they said?' and then, 'How did it happen?'

Martha did not answer and later she wondered, *Why did he even ask?* She knew he would have imagined it, exactly as it had occurred. He would have seen it all, vivid with his mind's eye: the crying child, the broken sleep and the open gate on the stairs.

I woke up and she was crying –

Martha was asked to describe what had happened – how it had happened – so many times that it became a story, and one that always began the same way. She learned where to breathe, just as if she were making a speech.

First she told the men from the ambulance, crouched at the bottom of the stairs. Then, at the hospital, she was asked to start again: *I woke up and she was crying.* Val pushed through the swinging doors with a crumbling, quake-struck face, and Martha told her too. Uniforms, stethoscopes, clipboards and lapel badges all stepped up to be told. When she finished – each time – they went away again. Doctors, nurses, specialists and then – *What?* – a social worker. A psycho-someone, and then another. Martha began to lose track.

She noticed that although she had arrived in the noisiest part of the hospital – *It's an emergency* – she was soon, somehow, in a quiet place. Nothing here seemed about to happen fast. There was no confusing wall of noise. Aside from the *flick-flap* of a door and the squeak of a rubber shoe there were only two sounds to speak of: the *mip-mip-mip* of one machine, and the regular *click-shush* of another.

All these people asked to hear it over and over again: *What? How? And then what?* When Martha reached the end there would be someone else, someone new, who needed to know from the start.

She was almost mad with fear, but afraid of sounding mad. She tried to make herself sensible, or at least to sound sensible, but it was hard – it was so hard that she began to wonder if perhaps she had gone mad. She could not seem to get a grip on herself. Was this what insanity was?

It was hours – the night was over and it was day – before she realised what they suspected: not that she was mad, but that she had hurt Eliza.

She said nothing at all after that.

When at last she spoke again it was to Clive: 'Don't you want me to be punished?'

In bed, they were lying on their backs and looking up. They could not seem to move closer together or further apart but only to lie with this fixed distance between them, like two railway sleepers.

'You're punishing yourself,' Clive said. 'It was an accident.'

It was not an answer to her question but he had told Martha what she wished to know. When she shut her eyes she saw a row of black-capped judges who shook their heads and pronounced her guilty. It was easy to recognise Clive, sitting in the midst of them.

Martha was too feeble to contain herself, here in the cottage alone, and what was the point in self-government? She made a little comma of her body in the bed, and rubbed her cheek with the pillow. As if she had given herself a signal, tears spilled from her eyes. All those marbles in her palm – accident, incident, blunder or crime – tumbled from her grasp and rolled away.

After lying awake all night – flat on his back like a felled tree – Clive got up, dressed, and surrendered.

'We'll leave after breakfast,' he said to Eliza.

'For the cottage?'

'Yes. Isn't that what you want?'

Eliza did not answer but asked a question of her own. 'Will Tom be there?'

'No. He's gone. It's just your mother and me.' Clive felt the weariness of defeat.

'You and Mum? *Huh.*' It was a new voice: a weapon as blunt as a hammer.

Clive looked at his daughter. 'That wasn't very nice.'

'Good.'

He could think of no reply to that and Val, wiping a dishrag over the counter, seemed not to have heard.

The sound of a car on the track wrung Martha from her bed. Upright – or near enough – she staggered to the window. She stubbed her toe but even that sharp pain did not dislodge the headache from her temples. She must have drunk some wine the night before.

A stranger's car – small, clean and white – was creeping up the track. Bother! How awkward.

Martha looked down at herself and found she was still dressed in yesterday's clothes. Pieces of the day fell into her mind: *Eliza safe – Tom gone – red wine.* The recollection made her swallow.

Downstairs she opened the kitchen door and found a neat man with an apologising face. 'I've come to have a look in your roof,' he said. 'For the bats?' He showed Martha a laminated identity card.

'Oh!' said Martha. 'I didn't know . . . '

'I had an appointment? With someone called Eliza Barkes?'

237

Tears threatened; Martha gulped. 'She's not here.' *Because she ran away.* 'But come in.'

They climbed the stairs to the attic door and Martha clicked the latch. 'It's a bit of a mess,' she apologised.

The man got out a torch. 'Everyone's is,' he said with a sigh.

Martha scrambled in after him and they crouched beside each other on the rafters, staring into the gloom.

Under the sorrowful beam of the torch a misshapen and half-remembered landscape of junk-filled boxes stretched away. Everything in here was degenerating into a clogged heap the colour and texture of pipe tobacco. Martha's heart sank to look at it.

Into the attic had been posted everything that she and Clive had no use for, but could not throw away. Her father's clothes and the manuscripts which she had never read. Broken Christmas tree lights. Boxes of records, cassettes, CDs and videotapes. Equipment that marked the beginning and end of self-improvement: diet books, juicers, dumb bells and weighing scales. Eliza's old school uniforms, her outgrown shoes and even that detested helmet, issued by the hospital, which made her scream until her parents took it off.

These things were meaningless now, but to look at them filled Martha with despair. Nothing could ever be got rid of. Even if something were carted away for trash it would still exist somewhere, buried in a hole or shredded into bits.

'Are they still here?' she asked her companion. 'Will they come back?'

'They're going to keep coming back,' he said, 'but does it matter?' He pointed the beam of the torch into the crevices above their heads. 'They were here all along, after all – you just didn't know about them.'

Martha sat back on her heels and considered. She could find nothing to argue with. 'It doesn't matter, does it?' she said. 'It's perfectly fine.' A sudden exhaustion – weakness – resignation – made her want to laugh. It was so quiet and warm up here. She smiled, yawned, felt hungry and thought of Eliza, travelling home. 'My daughter will be very pleased,' she said.

When the man had gone Martha found her telephone and got back into bed to use it. She propped herself up on the pillows and her heart thumped with nerves.

'Eliot?'

She would begin like this, but had not thought how to go on.

Afterwards she sat in the silence and stared out of the window. This day seemed to have many beginnings. She rested, pillowed by a new feeling of calm, before getting to her feet and starting again: undressing, washing, dressing, drinking coffee and finally taking the lamp from Eliza's bedside and moving it into the attic. She attached it to an extension cord and plugged it in on the landing, and then she climbed back into the roof and switched it on. Everything seemed to wince – to shrink back into its shell – but Martha would not be put off. She stared at it all with folded arms and a fierce look, and then she got to work.

Later – her eyes and nose clogged with dust and a rummaging pain in her back – she went down to the kitchen and

239

made herself a fried-egg sandwich. She ate it sitting on her father's bench, in the garden.

Tom liked to sit here and smoke as her father had done. Martha wondered whether Tom was with Eliot – perhaps they had woken up together in that empty, echoing Hampstead house.

The morning's activities had brought a welcome peace, and now Martha could think of both Tom and Eliot – of everyone – with equanimity. She stretched out her legs and looked down at the field. It was warm, here in this corner where the sun kissed the bench all day, and it felt a long way from London, Paris, or anywhere else she might be.

What will happen? This had been Eliza's question and now Martha asked it musingly of herself. Getting no answer she turned up her face to quiz the air, the tree and the skating swallows. *What will happen?*

She still sat in that spot, face tilted to the sun, when Clive's car drew in at the gate. At the sight her heart expanded with welcome.

Today, Martha guessed, Eliza would jump out of the car and run up the field to the house. Yes, here she came now: zigzagging with her arms outstretched and her palms brushing the tall, feathery tips of the grass.

Martha got to her feet, raised an arm and called out, 'Eliza!' The shout was instinctive: *Mine!* In a moment her daughter was wrapped in her arms and Martha said, 'Don't run away, never again, please. I was so frightened.'

Eliza did not answer but said, 'Ow, Mum, you're *hurting*.' She hinged herself out of the embrace. 'Has anything happened?' she asked. 'Has anyone been?'

'The bat man,' said Martha. 'He came especially to see you.' She heard the note of supplication in her voice and was surprised. *I am trying to appease*, she thought. With a sudden feeling of fright she knew that her authority had gone. Eliza had taken it with her, yesterday on the train, and had not delivered it back.

'What did he say?'

'He said they'll keep coming back and we ought to get used to it. He said they've been here, all these years, and we just didn't know.'

'That's what I said to Dad! See, Dad?' She turned to Clive. 'It's their home too.'

Martha turned to Clive and when she saw his face, in her mellow forgiving mood, her heart flared a little in pity – *Oh! You!* – as if she had brushed together the sweepings of love and put a match to them.

But Clive was not listening. 'Why are you covered in dust?' he asked Martha.

Martha patted her head. 'Oh,' she said. 'Because of the attic. I've been sorting out some of the rubbish up there.'

Eliza examined her. 'It looks cool,' she said. 'Like a witch or a ghost.'

Martha heard approval in that voice and felt the touch of loving tendrils reach around her heart. She was almost dizzy with relief, smiling and dazed, but then felt suddenly awkward – exposed – in front of Clive. 'You could help,' she suggested to him, for something to say. 'You could bring down some boxes.'

Clive did not want to commit. 'I'll come and take a look,' he said.

Following him up the stairs, Martha wondered if they would always speak to one another – perhaps for the rest of their lives – as if they were two strangers on a train who agreed that the weather was wet and the carriage unusually crowded. But how should she proceed? Should she shake a fist in Clive's face, stamp her foot and say, *Listen to me: I kissed a boy! Eliza ran away! Be mindful of us!* Was it safe to go on as if nothing had occurred, with independent thoughts and plans growing like weeds in the cracks between them? She felt as alert and trembling as one of those tall grasses in the field. *We are separate after all,* she thought. She felt a premonition throb in her heart and quake the length of her body. *We were a family, but today we are three.*

When Clive saw that a light had been lit in the attic he said, 'That doesn't look very safe.' He switched it off at the wall. 'What's wrong with using a torch?'

Martha felt very tired. 'There's nothing *wrong* with it,' she said, 'I just didn't.' She passed Clive a torch. 'Here – you have this. I'll fetch another.'

When she came back Clive was bent over one of the boxes marked 'Dump'. He had unsealed and opened it.

'What are you doing?' Martha asked him.

'Checking. In case there's something I want.'

'Oh, Clive, please don't.'

'Look,' he said in triumph, 'What's wrong with this?' He pulled out a kite and its tangled knot of string.

Standing on the grass, Eliza stretched out her arms as far as they would reach and began to rotate. This was the way to make her head spin: she felt her thoughts mix and stir into a muddle.

She tipped back her head and watched a swallow dip and swerve its open-hearted path across the blue. Like the bats, the swallows would not stay. They had somewhere else to be.

That fragile feeling began to creep into her limbs again. She thought of the delicate life of Hector Fox. Heads were easily hurt: she pictured an egg in boiling water, and the banner of white that would bloom from a tiny crack.

Yesterday, on the way to find Eliot, Eliza had asked her grandmother, 'What will happen, after today? Will it go back to normal?'

Val thought of a better question than an answer: 'What do you want to happen?'

No one had asked her this. Eliza realised, to her surprise, that she did not know the answer. She frowned, thinking it over.

A newspaper blew past them along the pavement and was scattered into pages by the wind. Eliza felt sorry to look at it, and suddenly she knew: 'I want all of us together,' she said. 'And I want Eliot too. She's my friend.' It was simple.

Val reached for Eliza's hand. 'Well,' she said. 'There's nothing too hard about that.'

It was a long, tall hill up to Eliot's house, and they held hands all the way, pulling each other along.

Back at the cottage, Eliza felt bigger.

Aren't you grown-up.

Yes I am.

The adventure of yesterday – all that she'd learned – had expanded her.

She was beginning to feel sick but it did not stop her turning. Stopping would be worse – the world would spin by itself. She shut her eyes and drew slow, gliding circles on the grass. Alternate patches of light and shade dabbed at her closed eyelids. In the sun her vision turned to orange; under the blot of the tree there was nothing but black. Perhaps she would lose track of her position and twirl out of the garden and into the field or the sky; perhaps she would open her eyes and find herself high above the grass, the house and the tree –

She heard a car door slam and stopped her revolutions to stand still. The inside of her head churned and so did her stomach. She staggered, blinked, gulped and tried to pin her wandering gaze on something fixed.

There was Eliot: standing in the yard beside her little car. She was looking straight at Eliza, with that rare smile on her face.

'Eliot!' Eliza ran to greet her.

From inside the house, Clive and Martha heard Eliza's exclamation: 'Eliot!'

Clive straightened his back and stood alerted, listening. He

244

went quite still, as if he had heard a frightening noise in the dark. Then he said to Martha, 'How did she find us?'

Martha had straightened up too. She was watching Clive. 'I told her we were here,' she said.

Clive looked at her, disbelieving. 'What?'

'I talked to her.' She waited a moment and then answered a question he had not asked. 'It was the right thing to do.' Sounding peaceable, calm and collected she went on, 'Eliza, me, your mother, Tom – we all trust her, Clive.' She spoke with decision: *we have settled this matter without you.* 'It's what Eliza wants. She never did anything wrong.'

Was this Eliza or Eliot, who had never done anything wrong? Clive wanted to stop Martha – *Stop!* – and to contradict her – *No!* – and then to beg for a pause from time itself – *Wait!* –

But Eliza's bold voice called up the stairs from the hall: 'Hey, Mum? Guess what: Eliot's here.'

Clive could picture his daughter swinging from the latch, just as she had since the day that she could reach it. Here was the pause he had wanted: for a moment he allowed the luxury of that image, now outgrown, to dab at his mind with its soft, remembered colours.

'I'm coming down,' Martha called. She turned to Clive. 'Well?' It was almost a challenge. 'What about you?'

But Clive could not respond. He did not move.

A moment of stillness – a question and an answer in the air – and then Martha turned and stepped down into the house. Confident, light-footed, she continued down the stairs with a free, careless stride that Clive could only envy. 'I'm coming,' her voice sang out again. 'Are you in the garden?' He heard a door slam.

In the thick, closeted air Clive waited and listened. The attic itself was a hood which muffled his head. He strained to hear any sound, any sign, that might help him. A tumble of boxes, some of them opened, were balanced on the beams around him. *I should have left all this alone*, he realised.

A laugh: Eliza's. The slam of two car doors. An engine sparking, coughing and stammering into life.

Clive's head swam. He found his feet and pounded down the stairs to the garden door. 'Eliza? Martha?' No one answered. With a kicking heart in his chest he ran across the garden and into the yard.

The car was perched at the lip of the yard and ready to leave. Eliot sat in the driving seat and Eliza waved from beside her. Martha, on her feet and smiling, waved back. Clive raised his own hand – *Stop!* – but now they were off: pelting away down the track in a clatter and spit of stones, pausing at the lane – the *clunk-rev* of a changing gear – and now they were gone.

'Where are they going?' Clive's voice was dry with dust and fright.

'Just for a spin in the car – Eliza's been longing to go.' Martha folded her arms and spoke with a kind of defiance. 'I wanted to go with them, but there wasn't room.' Turning to Clive she examined his expression. 'What's the matter?' She peered at him closely. 'Clive?'

But Clive did not respond. He put a hand up to his brow,

and looked across the field. A pitiless wind beat at his face; it hurt his eyes to search this empty view.

'Clive?' Martha said again. She glanced from his face to the horizon and back again. 'There's nothing there.'

She was right – Clive knew she must be right – but he did not want to be told.

Martha turned away from him, to the house. 'Are you coming?'

'Not yet.'

He stayed where he was, watching. Only the lifting spirals of dust, circling into the air, told him that the little car had ever come or gone.

Eliot drove fast: the passing hedge was a dark green blur. The car's roof was down, and the windows rolled wide open.

Eliza's hair, head and whole body were buffeted by the scented summer air. It was delicious and exciting. She raised her hands above her head for a moment, daring herself, and then she turned to Eliot. 'It feels like we're flying,' she said. 'It feels like we're free.'

Eliot seemed to take this remark very seriously. When, after a moment or two, she smiled across at Eliza she looked quite different. 'That's how I feel too,' she said.